*The Innocence
of the Devil*

LITERATURE OF THE MIDDLE EAST

*a series of fiction, poetry, and memoirs
in translation*

)

TITLES PUBLISHED AND IN PRESS

Memoirs from the Women's Prison, by Nawal El Saadawi
translated by Marilyn Booth

Arabic Short Stories
translated by Denys Johnson-Davies

The Innocence of the Devil, by Nawal El Saadawi
translated by Sherif Hetata

Memory for Forgetfulness: August, Beirut, 1982
by Mahmoud Darwish
translated by Ibrahim Muhawi

Aunt Safiyya and the Monastery, by Bahaa' Taher
translated by Barbara Romaine

NAWAL EL SAADAWI

The Innocence of the Devil

Translated from the Arabic by
Sherif Hetata

With an Introduction by
Fedwa Malti-Douglas

University of California Press
Berkeley   Los Angeles

University of California Press
Berkeley and Los Angeles, California

First Paperback Printing 1998

Published by arrangement with Methuen London.

Library of Congress Cataloging-in-Publication Data
Sa‘ dāwī, Nawāl
    [Jannāt wa-Iblīs. English]
    The innocence of the Devil / Nawal El Saadawi ;
translated from the Arabic by Sherif Hetata ; introduction
by Fedwa Malti-Douglas.
        p. cm.
    Includes bibliographical references.
    ISBN 0-520-21652-0 (alk. paper : pbk.)
    I. Hatātah, Sharīf.   II. Malti-Douglas, Fedwa.   III. Title.
PJ7862.A3J3613   1994
892'.736—dc20   94-17128
                                                    CIP

Printed in the United States of America
9 8 7 6 5 4 3 2 1

The paper used in this publication is both acid-free and totally
chlorine-free (TCF). It meets the minimum requirements of
American Standard for Information Sciences—Permanence
of Paper for Printed Library Materials, ANSI Z39.48-1984. ∞

Contents

Introduction: From Theology to Rape   vii

1 Ganat Arrives   1

2 The First Session   14

3 Another Woman   30

4 Narguiss   38

5 A Fight in the Night   52

6 Nefissa   68

7 Ganat in a Moment of Consciousness   86

8 Guilt   104

9 And in the Beginning was the Serpent   130

10 Sinful Love   150

11 Nefissa Stops Calling Out   176

12 Ganat Breaks Out   198

13 The Innocence of the Devil   215

Introduction to The Innocence of the Devil: *From Theology to Rape*

by Fedwa Malti-Douglas

The Arab world's leading feminist and iconoclast: this is Nawal El Saadawi. Few Arab women inspire as much emotion or find themselves the subject of as much polemic. No Arab woman's pen has violated as many sacred enclosures. Her novel *The Innocence of the Devil* (the Arabic original is *Jannât wa-Iblîs,* the names of two of the central characters[1]), which addresses such diverse subjects as religion, sexuality, the body, and violation of the female by a male deity, is an important addition to her literary corpus.[2]

Nawal El Saadawi was born in 1931 in the village of Kafr Tahla in the Egyptian delta, attended public schools, and studied at the Faculty of Medicine at the University of Cairo. Her formal education, therefore, took place in native Egyptian Arabic-language schools. This is not insignificant as many Arab intellectuals have received a substantial proportion of their education either outside the region or in foreign (and generally foreign-language) schools in the Arab world. Nawal was not the only child in her family to attend college—all her siblings did as well. But El Saadawi did not choose to pursue medicine for its own sake; rather, the career chose her: as she puts it, "the Faculty of Medicine takes the best students, those with the highest grades." At the Faculty of Medicine, she was one of approximately fifty women among hundreds of men. She graduated in 1955 and practiced in the areas of thoracic medicine and psychiatry. El Saadawi was appointed to the Ministry of Health in 1958 but was dismissed from the ministry and her post as Egypt's national public health director in August 1972 due to her frank writings on sexuality, specifically in *Women and Sex*.[3]

The dangers that El Saadawi ran because of her uncompromising views became more dramatic in 1981, when she was imprisoned by the Egyptian president, Anwar Sadat, during his massive incarceration of Egyptian intellectuals. This period, though brief, had a powerful artistic impact on El Saadawi. She wrote *The Fall of the Imam*,[4] a novel which is heavily inspired by her experience under the Sadat regime and which helped place her name on the death lists circulated by conservative Islamist groups.

After her imprisonment Nawal El Saadawi founded the Arab Women's Solidarity Association (AWSA) in 1982, an international organization dedicated to "lifting the veil from the mind" of the Arab woman. In 1985, the association was granted "consultative status with the Economic and Social Council of the United Nations as an Arab non-governmental organization."[5] The AWSA organized conferences and weekly seminars and functioned as a locus for frank discussions of topics related to gender analysis or women's status. On June 15, 1991, the Egyptian government closed down the Arab Women's Solidarity Association and diverted its funds to a religious women's organization. El Saadawi, with her customary energy and conviction, took the Egyptian government to court, but to no avail. The association's magazine, *Nûn,* has also disappeared from public life.[6] El Saadawi chronicled this phase of the AWSA's saga in the volume *A New Battle in Woman's Cause.*[7]

These activities mark Nawal El Saadawi as perhaps the most visible woman intellectual in the Arab world. She has the dubious honor of supposedly being the only woman whose name has been placed on the Islamist death lists. Many Arab leftist intellectuals whose names appear on these lists have confidently declared to me that no Islamist group would ever kill a woman. After the 1992 assassination of the Egyptian secularist intellectual Faraj Fûda, however, El Saadawi began to take these threats against her life more seriously; she now divides her time between

Europe and the United States and makes frequent but brief visits to her native Egypt.

If there is a single activity that has sustained this Egyptian feminist throughout the stages of her life, in medical school, government employ, imprisonment, that activity is writing. El Saadawi takes great pride in relating the story of how she disposed of her second husband, a lawyer. When his colleagues complimented him on a short story his wife had published, he presented her with an ultimatum: choose between him or her writing. Her answer: "Well, I choose my writing."[8] This is a dramatic step for an Arab woman, for whom marriage still fulfills a socially sacred and legitimizing function. But such a choice should not surprise anyone who knows Nawal El Saadawi; the demons of writing inhabited her even as a child. At age thirteen, in 1944, she had already penned the novel *Memoirs of a Female Child Named Su'âd.*[9]

In the fifty years since authoring that childhood story, El Saadawi has written continuously and imposed herself on the world literary scene. Her latest novel, *Love in the Time of Oil,*[10] is the most recent work in an enormous corpus of fictional and nonfictional texts: medical treatises, short stories, novels, plays, prison memoirs, travelogues, critical essays. No other Arab woman author (and few Arab men) approaches El Saadawi in the breadth of her writing, and her study *The Hidden Face of Eve: Women in the*

Arab World is by now a classic in the West.[11] Genres aside, the Egyptian feminist has also never shied away from subjects other authors might not even consider writing about. Her literary obsessions, ranging as they do from male-female relations to physical gender boundaries, identify her as a literary iconoclast.

El Saadawi's imprisonment under Sadat inspired several works, which permitted the writer to enter fully into domains that she had previously only skirted. Thus *The Fall of the Imam,* with its patriarchal ruler (who is, among others, a stand-in for Sadat), weaves a tale that is an ambitious rewriting of patriarchy. In the Saadawian system, patriarchy is an all-inclusive system that informs social, political, and religious structures.

In *The Innocence of the Devil,* Nawal El Saadawi boldly continues the project begun with *The Fall of the Imam.* Here the religious intertext dominates, redefining the political and social structures with which it comes into contact. The setting is an insane asylum and Satan and God are confined side by side as patients. This novel is, like *The Fall of the Imam,* a narrative in which events repeat and characters intertwine with one another. Who is the Deity? Who is the Devil? This provocative Saadawian narrative redefines not only the relationship between God and the Devil (Eblis is one of the names of the Devil in Arabic) but that between Adam and Eve, between man and woman. Christianity and Islam are both guilty here, and the Devil, like woman, becomes but a victim of the patriarchal order. The body is a central player, with the physical rape of a woman only one of its articulations. Just as one cannot hope to comprehend the literary danger of *The Fall of the Imam* without understanding Islam (a devout Muslim called the book blasphemy in my presence), one cannot comprehend *The Innocence of the Devil,* a text based on close readings of the Islamic tradition, without understanding fundamental aspects of the three Abrahamic religions.

The Innocence of the Devil might seem to represent a departure from the author's previous texts. In her first mature work, *Memoirs of a Woman Doctor,* El Saadawi attempted to venture into the domain of religion but had her hand slapped by the censors, who excised what they perceived to be the offensive sections from the novel.[12] Gradually, she began probing this sensitive cultural area, testing the waters before fully jumping in with *The Innocence of the Devil.* Her task has been facilitated by political and civilizational factors outside her control. Her exploration of religion has been facilitated by the Islamist movement in the Middle East, a movement that has planted itself firmly in the region, with roots that go deeper than Western critics perceive. More secularized Arab writers and intellectuals, like El Saadawi, are aware of the cultural impact of this religious movement. El Saadawi responded with her own feminist interpretation of the centuries-old Arabo-Islamic textual corpus, and she did not enter the verbal battle unarmed: she read deeply and widely among the religious normative texts, such as the Koran and the Hadith, commentaries, and lives of the Prophets, as well as less religiously oriented textual materials.[13] The result, *The Innocence of the Devil,* is El Saadawi's tour-de-force novelistic foray into theology.

The novel includes one third-person narrator who remains cautiously outside the text. The third-person narration is perhaps the least difficult of the text's literary properties. Events move dizzyingly between past and present, fantasy and reality. Different levels of the language add to this ambiguity: the dialogue sometimes takes place in literary Arabic, at other times in Egyptian dialect, and in certain cases both levels of the language are involved at once.

A highly complex postmodern work, *The Innocence of the Devil* also relies on sophisticated intertextual games with some of the most sacred writings of the Islamic tradition. The remainder of this introduction sketches paths through these literary and cultural thickets. Those readers who prefer their suspense untinged by foreknowledge may wish to turn directly to the novel—they will certainly find it gripping and powerful—and this discussion will be waiting for them patiently if their curiosity has been whetted.

The Innocence of the Devil is set in a mental hospital. The character Ganat enters the enclosure on the first page of the text. The reader traverses the portal with her and, in the process, meets the cast of characters: Eblis (the Devil), an older man addressed as the Lord, a female patient named Nefissa, and the individuals in charge of the institution, including the male Director and female Head Nurse. The Director prescribes Ganat's treatment: residence in a solitary room under observation and three sessions of electroshock therapy a week.

For the reader, meeting the characters involves learning about their past lives, including interaction with family, schoolteachers, the religiopolitical system, and so on. The chapters center on different characters, and though there is a clear progression in the novel from beginning to end, this is not a linear progression.

For the majority of characters in *The Innocence of the Devil,* the asylum is not a locus that allows forward vision. Rather, it is a place where the past assumes center stage, governing and delimiting the actions of the individuals. Ganat thinks back to her grandfather, a Muslim, and her grandmother, a Christian who converted to Islam but retained her Christian beliefs. We hear about her school days and her more informal education at home, where the grandmother's popular religiosity and superstitions come to the surface.

When Ganat sets eyes on the Head Nurse, she asks, "Narguiss?" No, the Head Nurse shakes her head. But Ganat's intuition that the nurse is someone other than who she pretends to be is correct. Her identity? Narguiss, the daughter of a civil servant. She received the Medal of Nationalism and Honor, which she proudly wears on her person, even in the asylum. On her wedding night, she shed no blood. To erase this shame, her father committed suicide. The Director of the facility uses her body and when she tells him that though she was a virgin, she shed no blood, he reassures her that her hymen was elastic.

The reader discovers as the narrative progresses that Ganat's recognition of Narguiss was more than serendipity. The two once had a friendship that bordered on lesbianism. When a schoolteacher asked Narguiss whom she loved most in the world, she replied, "I love Ganat." Rumors began to fly about this sinful love caused by Eblis. Just as this hidden past is coming alive for Narguiss, however, Ganat forgets it and she is declared cured. Narguiss/the Head Nurse challenges the Director and reveals to him that she no longer wishes to have anything to do with men. When he confronts her with her lesbianism and curses her, she runs away and is transformed into a white butterfly. Another white butterfly joins her and the two are shot, ending their saga in drops of blood.

Nefissa, the third woman whose past unfolds before us in the asylum, is said to be Eblis's sister. After all, had she not as a child heard the male teacher, Sheikh Masoud, call her brother Eblis? Nefissa's past is intimately tied to her mother, who lost her son in a religiopolitical movement. He, along with other young men, was recruited to fight, only to die. The mother is told that her son is in Heaven with his Lord, in the Garden of Eden with prophets and martyrs. As Nefissa thinks about these events, and about her own journey to Cairo to look for her lost brother, she repeatedly utters the invocation, "O God." She is looking out the window of the women's ward, and who should hear her but the Deity in the hospital who commands her to "come down." The Deity questions her about her virtue and then asks her to declare herself his servant. This she does, provoking yet more questions about his being the only man in her life, without consort. Satisfied with her answers, he proceeds to rape her. Her scream rouses the medical staff of the asylum, who then escort the culprit to the "electricity room," one assumes for electroshock therapy.

This Deity creates this relationship not only with Nefissa. He had earlier demonstrated that he was inextricably tied to Eblis as well. He wakes Eblis in the middle of the night and urges him to go out and do his duty—whispering to people and tempting them. Eblis, wishing to sleep, tries to dissuade the Deity, but without success; he finally decides to kiss the Deity's head out of respect. He jumps out of bed, knocking the turban from the master's head and provoking what looks to the other inmates like a fistfight between Eblis and the Lord. An individual with a book under his arm appears to set up a tribunal. He is a judge, whose activities come to an end only when the asylum siren sounds, bringing with it the medical staff.

The intimate relationship between the Lord and his antithesis, Eblis, reaches a climax at the novel's end. Eblis is now deceased and the Deity's remorse is beyond compare, to the point that the Deity himself is discovered dead at the close of the text. Before his demise, however, he has in vain declared Eblis's innocence: "Forgive me, my son. You are innocent." The last words he utters are "Innocent! Innocent!"

Why an insane asylum? Placing patients in such a setting and subjecting them to electroshock therapy is not unusual in fiction, especially among women writers. Here the asylum permits the unfolding of complicated literary games, not the least important of which is the game of fantasy and reality. Once Ganat has crossed the portal of the hospital, bringing the reader with her, the rules of the reality game change. The reader knows that characters who inhabit this peculiar world may not be subject to the same regulations and dynamics under which the world outside the institution operates. The incarceration of this Deity and his cohorts in the asylum permits innovative transgressions and violations, the most subversive of which involve theology. Since the reader enters the enclosed literary space on the first page of the novel, all subsequent narrative acts, whether inside or outside the asylum, are colored by the confinement.

Theology is by far the most consistent undercurrent in both the pre-asylum and the post-asylum lives of the characters, providing the subtext for the entirety of *The Innocence of the Devil*. It governs the names, the relationships, the gender dynamics, the linguistic system. By virtue of this enormous textual power, it also permits the creation of irony, wordplay, and the like.

For example, when the newcomer is first asked her name, she replies, "Ganat." She is fond of her name, the plural of *Paradise*. When she was asked what this name meant, her grandfather (or her father) opened "the book" and read:

—The *Gana* of Eden in which flow rivers of honey and milk.

She did not like the taste of honey, nor that of milk, and preferred salted cheese or pickles. (19)

The dynamics have been presented. Ganat's name, her onomastic identity, has been defined in terms of the Muslim Holy Book.

Rivers of milk and honey are some of the pleasures awaiting the believer in the Muslim Paradise. The Koran speaks in many places of rivers flowing in Paradise.[14] These liquids of Muslim Paradise are discussed in detail by later Koranic commentators and are considered different from the same-name products existing in this world, whose nature changes. The paradisiacal liquids will have been created ex nihilo in the rivers. The milk, for example, does not come from animals and the purified honey differs from the honey of this world, mixed as it is with beeswax.[15] More interesting, the Holy Book in the context of rivers also speaks of *jannât* (gardens or paradises), identical to the character's name in the novel.[16]

The narrator denudes this religious intertext of any of its possible metaphorical connotations with the statement that the young woman did not like the taste of honey and milk. Opposed to these two sweet and particularly significant fluids are solid foods, both of which are distinguished by the strength of their taste—salted cheese and pickles. The name *Ganat* recasts the entire concept of Paradise.

It is not simply the plurality of the gardens inherent in Ganat's name that links her directly to the religious domain. Lying in the coffin, Ganat sees her official name: Ganat Abd Allah Abdil Illah. She asks herself whether Abd Allah is her father's name and Abdil Illah that of her grandfather. Her memory awakens gradually. She hears her grandmother calling out to her grandfather: *"Abdil Illat."* He jumped up and corrected her: *"Abdil Illah* not *Abdillat."* Her grandmother consistently changed the *h* to a *t,* and her grandfather just as consistently tried to correct her. *"Illah* not *Illat."* He grabbed his wife's hand and tried to make her write the two letters, the *h* and the *t,* which look identical but for the two dots over the *t.* "The feminine has two dots on it." Ganat, while asleep, heard her grandmother repeating the mistake. Her grandfather's voice rang out in the night: "The two dots, you she-ass!" Her grandmother's response? "Making a history out of two dots. Turning the world upside down just because of two dots. God take you from this world" (200–201).

The two dots on which this entire discussion hinges are not so innocuous. True, if one remains merely in the domain of Arabic grammar and lexicography, the two dots signal the feminine gender. When the grandfather declares that the "feminine has two dots on it," he is correct, but only on one level. Lest the reader miss the other connotations of this discussion, the narrator continues. The ever-curious Ganat asks her grandmother whether Allah is different from Al Illah. "I don't know," replies the old woman. "Ask

your father and your grandfather." Ganat does, up-
setting her grandfather: "I take refuge in thee, o God,
from the sinful Devil." We next see Ganat being
made to write three times: *"I take refuge in thee, o God,
. . . I take refuge in. . . ."* When she finally gets out the
third *h*, two ink drops fall on the page, turning the *h*
into a *t*. It is again as if the world were overturned.
The schoolteacher Sheikh Bassiouni looks at her
notebook and loses control, shouting, *"I take refuge in
Al Illah! I take refuge in Al Illah!"* He raps Ganat on
the knuckles and erases the dots so hard that he rips
the paper. When his eyes spotted the two dots, it was
"as though he were seeing Eblis in person, and not
two dots of ink." He made the school girls recite after
him a Koranic verse: *"And dids't thou witness Illat and
El Ouza and Manat who is their third. And shalt thou
have the male, and he the female. That is indeed an unjust
way to apportion them out."* He stared at the girls and
continued: *"Those who do not believe in the forever after
do call the angels by female names."* (202–4).

Ganat has indeed opened up a can of worms. Her
inquiries that innocently began in the domain of language end up in that of theology. The Arabic language itself has done nothing but facilitate her task.
The word *Allâh,* as is well known, is composed of two
elements: the definite article *al* (the), and the word for
"deity," *ilâh,* the entirety elided into al-Lâh or Allâh,
the Deity par excellence. To complicate matters, the

pronunciation of this word varies according to the vowel that precedes it. If it is preceded by the *i,* as in *aʿûdhu bil-Lâh* (I seek God's protection)—the phrase we hear repeated over and over again by the male characters in this segment of the text—then the pronunciation is with an open *a,* bringing it close to the *al-Lâh* that Ganat inquires about. From there, it is an easy jump to *al-Lât,* a word in which the *h,* when written, picks up those two infamous dots, transforming *al-Lâh* into *al-Lât.* Grammar has transported the reader into the domain of theology.

On a most rudimentary level, Ganat and her grandmother have transformed a grammatically male deity into a grammatically female one. (It should be remembered that though the word *Allâh* is grammatically masculine, Muslim theologians have always argued that human categories such as gender do not apply to God.) Furthermore, these are not just any two deities. The female, al-Lât, is one of the pre-Islamic goddesses, who, along with her female cohorts, surfaces in the Koranic verse recited by Sheikh Bassiouni.[17] It was the elimination of these pagan deities that the Prophet Mohammed set out to accomplish in the seventh century. Islam is a monotheistic religion, one of whose central precepts is the notion of *tawhîd,* the unity and transcendence of Allâh. How sacrilegious it is then that the women play these gender games with male and female deities! Not only is doubt cast on the nature of the Deity, but in the process one of the pre-Islamic goddesses has been unwittingly revived.

Is it a wonder that the two individuals who respond to this impertinence are both males, the grandfather and the schoolteacher? Both react with frustration and impatience. For both, the confusion between the two letters turns the world upside down, leading to verbal and physical abuse of the females.

This abuse of women is clearly linked to the domain of religion. But it is the Deity in the asylum who performs the ultimate violation of the female—rape. When the Deity, answering Nefissa's call, beckons her to come down, she does so. He takes her hand and leads her to a dark corner of the garden. She has kept her eyes closed, in keeping with Sheikh Masoud's advice that "if she opened her eyes she would be struck blind by the powerful light" (82). During the interrogation leading to the rape, the Lord asks her to kneel and say "I am your obedient slave." As she does so and takes his hand, the narrator notes that his hand is "smoother than the hand of the Village Headman. His nails were clean, carefully clipped. But in his clothes was a smell of sweat. Did God sweat like human beings? Her doubts did not last for more than a moment" (83).

Clearly, Nefissa believes that the man she is dealing with is the Deity. When she responds to his questions, she includes in every answer the words *my Lord* or *my God*. She is affirming to herself and to the reader that she believes she is indeed involved with the Deity. After all, she heeds Sheikh Masoud's words, based as they are on a real belief in the blinding power of the vision of God.

The perspiration, a sure sign of the corporality of the being in question, only causes her to hesitate for a moment; it should cause the reader to pause for a longer period. The narrator with this simple phrase has effectively called the reality of Nefissa's world into question. What is the certainty that returns to her? For her, it is that this man really is the Deity, but the reader should by now know better. The manipulation of the gullible female is real, as is her rape. Had she opened her eyes, had she herself doubted what Sheikh Masoud told her about the blinding power of the light, she might have averted the rape.

This woman-victim is an inmate of the institution, along with the Deity. His reality, it could be argued, is hers. Yet what about the texture of his hands and the fact of his perspiration? The narrator compares the hand of the "Lord" to that of the Headman. These corporal comparisons are not innocent. When Nefissa asks herself the question of whether or not the Lord perspires like other humans, she has, without realizing it, tumbled on an important theological issue that long plagued Muslim thinkers and revolved around the question of God's attributes. The anthropomorphic description of the Deity was vigorously debated in the Middle Ages, and it was Ahmad ibn Hanbal, founder of the most conservative legal school in Islam, who declared that these corporal attributes were to be understood *bi-lâ kayf* (without how).[18]

Of course, when the question was debated among the medieval Muslims, the physical attributes of the Deity were more noble ones than perspiration (such as sitting on a throne). Although this bodily function has as its primary result the creation of doubt in Nefissa's mind, it does much more for the discerning reader. It ridicules the theological discussions over God's attributes and reminds us that should the Deity possess these attributes in the first place, then he would be a corporeal being who along with sitting on a throne would undoubtedly perspire as well.

Does this mean that the narrator is turning Nefissa into an advocate of Islamic theology? No. The narrator is playing an infinitely more delicate game. What we learn is that woman and theology are an explosive mixture. Nefissa is doubly the victim of male authority figures: on one level the Sheikh, on another level the Deity.

Nefissa's molestation, like that of other Saadawian female heroes, is embedded in an additional referential universe, this time that of theology.[19] Before the actual physical assault, the Deity subjects the woman-victim to two interrogations. Not surprisingly, in each of these instances, the incarcerated Deity touches on major cultural and civilizational forces.

The first line of questioning involves Nefissa's relationship with Eblis. Is she a pious woman? Has Eblis whispered anything to her? Has he visited her or she him? Nefissa passes this examination. The association of woman with the Devil, Eblis, is not innocent. In the Arabo-Islamic imagination, woman and the Devil are a lively pair, at times becoming synonymous with each other. Numerous are the references to their intimate association, and these range from religious normative material to the more secular poetic and proverbial corpus.[20] The construct that brings woman close to Eblis and his kingdom of Hellfire in the Arabo-Islamic textual unconscious continues to the present day and helps the twentieth-century reader understand the contemporary dialogue into which *The Innocence of the Devil* has inserted itself.[21]

Nefissa's second interrogation involves the Deity more directly. Is she going to be his obedient wife? Is he the first man in her life? Is he the one without a partner (the only one)? No human or spirit? "I need proof of that." The Deity's inquiries are seemingly directed at first glance to Nefissa's relations with other males, a "partner" referring to Nefissa's other sexual exploits. But this question leads the reader to more theologically complicated issues. As soon as the Deity has uttered the word *sharîk* (partner), he has himself entered the domain of theological debate in Islam over God's unity. To provide the Deity with a partner *(sharîk)* is to draw away from his unity *(taw-hîd)*, lapsing into idolatry *(shirk)*, the most serious transgression in Islam.[22] Nefissa seems oblivious to these larger issues. She merely parrots the Deity's questions but in an affirmative fashion.

Following this interrogation, the Deity proceeds to the proof. Nefissa, with eyes closed, feels her *gallabeya* going up and his fingers crawling on her body.

> The beating beneath her ribs came to a stop. She murmured the opening verse of the Koran.[23]
> —He is the one everlasting God.
> Then suddenly she felt something searing like a flame.(84)

Nefissa's recitation of the Koranic verse confirms the theological nature of the second interrogation. What she mutters under her breath are the first two verses of the Sûrat al-Ikhlâs (a chapter from the Koran) that ascertain the unity of the Deity, juxtaposing the all-important theological notion with corporal violence against women. The word for flame or fire, here *al-nâr*, simultaneously denotes fire and Hellfire.

The two interrogations, the first involving Eblis and the second involving the Deity himself, followed by the rape, function on two levels, one textual and the other metaphorical. In the world of the asylum where the women coexist with the Devil and the Deity, it might not seem out of line to question Nefissa about her relations with different males. But El Saadawi's novel is speaking to two readers: on the one hand, those staying on the surface of the text and following a woman's victimization, and on the other hand, those able to discern a deeper feminist theological commentary.

The Deity's rape of Nefissa links the theological and the sexual. Monotheism, the concern of the male patriarchal establishment, is transmuted into an obsession that expresses itself through sexual jealousy. The female is but a pawn in this game, her body having to bear the burden of proof.

The Muslim Deity is not the only inhabitant of the gendered religious universe of *The Innocence of the Devil*. Women as a collectivity raise the specter of that other Deity, the Yahweh of the Old Testament. All three Abrahamic religions seem to coexist here, but they coexist in a distinct hierarchy; clearly, the preference is for Islam. At the same time, however, Islam seems to be the property of the male and of the patriarchal system.

The rape by the Deity is symptomatic of an aspect of male-female relations that the narrator presents but also seems to undermine and subvert. These are the normal power relationships in which the male dominates the female. Ganat's grandmother is a case in point. The grandfather believes he has been successful in his attempt to convert her to his religion, but the reader knows the depth of his illusion.

The character of the Head Nurse is extremely significant here. When we first meet her, she is under the control of the Director of the facility. His power is both sexual and professional. At the outset, she seems to meet all the criteria for the perfect sellout: she works within the system, wears its medal on her person, tries to emulate the smiles of male leaders, refuses to admit her identity to her childhood friend. Her official mask as the Head Nurse seems complete.

Soon, however, cracks begin to appear in this mask. The medal the Head Nurse receives is the Medal of Nationalism and Honor. Yet honor is precisely the element that brings tragedy to her life. On Narguiss/the Head Nurse's wedding night, the midwife should have been able to extricate the blood from the broken hymen, but none appeared. Honor, the narrator is quick to tell us, is the honor of males, with females acting as its evidence or proof. Narguiss/the Head Nurse's father killed himself over this shame. She lifts her eyes, filled with tears, to the sky. "Her father was better than the Prophet Abraham. He had sacrificed himself for his daughter" (49). This revelation is that of the Head Nurse, not the narrator. It comes to her as she calls up the image of Abraham about to slaughter his son before the appearance of the scapegoat.

Narguiss/the Head Nurse should have been killed when her honor was cast into doubt, but she was not. One of her functions seems to be precisely the questioning and subverting of these traditional values. Her task may be facilitated by the fact that she, unlike her female colleagues in the text, is outwardly a functioning female member of the male establishment. There is an intimate paradigmatic relationship between her absent corporal honor and the symbolic medal of honor she wears.

The ultimate subversion by Narguiss/the Head Nurse involves her sexual preference. When Ganat's cure is declared successful, the Director fills out the official papers and hands the order to the Head Nurse. But she does not extend her hand to take the order. She had done that for thirty years: "For thirty years she had stood with bent head, unable to lift her eyes to him." This time, she lifts her head and stares at the Director's eyes.

—What's the matter with you, girl? Why are you standing like a statue?
—My name is Narguiss, not girl.
—Since when?

He lifted his hand and brought his cane down on her breast.

—Since when, you girl?

—From now onwards.

—Prepare the beer and the snacks. I'm coming to see you tonight.

—I'm leaving, leaving everything.

—Where are you going? To another man?

—I hate you. I hate all men.

—You love women now, eh?

—Yes.

—You'll go to Hellfire with Lot's people.[24]

—No, sir, I won't.

—To be a lesbian is a sin, don't you know that?

—No, sir. It is not mentioned in God's book.

—You fallen woman. (172–73)

This confrontation between the Head Nurse/Narguiss and the male Director goes directly to the heart of the matter. The Head Nurse's first step in asserting herself is to establish her identity: she is not "girl," she now has a name, Narguiss. This earns her a physical beating from the Director. His attempt to reestablish their relationship in its previous dynamics of master and servant fails. His last card is to inquire about other men, obviously unable to see a woman in other than purely heterosexual terms. Narguiss's reply takes him by surprise. Yes, she loves women. Naming, a process that provides an individual with identity, does more than that here; it also permits Narguiss to declare openly her sexual preference.

Once Narguiss's attraction to the same sex is declared, the dialogue shifts registers. Up to that point, it was dominated by the discourse of social power and male-female interaction. Then it enters the religio-theological realm in which the game of power will be shifted. The mention of Hell and the people of Lot is the signal: "Lot's people" is a reference to male homosexuality and refers to verses in the Koran in which Lot's followers are linked to male homosexual desire. The narrator has already sensitized the reader to this issue when the boy (Eblis) mistakenly recites the verse from the Koran about Lot and his followers: "And Lot, when he said to his people . . . ' . . . you approach men lustfully instead of women; no, you are a people that do exceed."[25]

Male homosexuality earned its practitioners a place in Hell,[26] but this does not indicate its complete omission in the literary culture.[27] The Director assumes that the punishment is identical for lesbianism. Narguiss's vehemence in responding to his comment is eloquent: "No, sir." Not deterred, he then declares that lesbianism is unlawful. Narguiss will not be fooled: "No, sir. It is not mentioned in God's book." Narguiss shows herself to be a worthy opponent, indeed. She is quite aware that the Muslim Holy Book makes no mention of female homosexuality.[28]

The interchange between Narguiss and her male opponent permits her to correct his misperception about female homosexuality. The game of power has shifted, and Narguiss now has the theological upper hand. The proof? When she declares that the topic of lesbianism is not in the Book of God, she changes linguistic registers. Up to this point, her interchange with the Director had been in the Egyptian dialect. This last sentence she utters in literary Arabic, which alerts the Director (and the reader) to the importance of her statement. The Director's response: "You fallen woman."

Ganat as a fallen woman is linked to her mother, Eve. When the narrator makes it clear that man can fall only in elections, military battles, or school examinations, the last recourse is to Adam. Adam and Eve: the male-female couple whose sojourn in the Garden of Eden and whose fall from grace are crucial to the mental structures of all three Abrahamic religions. True, Islam does not lay the blame for the Fall squarely at Eve's door, Adam being responsible as well.[29] Yet in a certain misogynistic strand of the Islamic religiocultural system, Eve carries the blame.[30]

Ganat's grandmother read to her the biblical story of Eve and the serpent, from the Christian perspective. On the Muslim side, Narguiss's father explained to her mother that the Lord forgave Adam only. The Koranic verse is cast in the singular, not the dual, although in previous verses, the dual reference was used.

The Saadawian narrator has stumbled or walked

on purpose into a vigorously debated issue in Arabo-Islamic texts. Did God, after the Fall, forgive only Adam, or did He forgive both Adam and Eve? The Koranic citation in question is from the Sûrat al-Baqara (The Sûra of the Cow). The events in the Holy Book begin with God's enjoining Adam and Eve to live in the Garden of Eden and not to partake of the tree. Satan leads the two astray, causing the Deity to cast them out. All these actions take place in the grammatical dual, referring to both Adam and Eve. Then the first part of verse 37 of Sûrat al-Baqara reads, "Thereafter Adam received certain words from his Lord, and He turned towards him,"[31] meaning that the Deity forgave him. There is no grammatical ambiguity here: the pronominal suffixes are in the masculine singular.

When first posing the problem, the Saadawian text reverses the Koranic passage from the Sûrat al-Baqara. Instead, Narguiss's father explains to his wife that "God had listened to what Adam had to say and had forgiven him alone" (116). Male actors are reversed: in the original text, Adam is the recipient of the words, whereas in the contemporary feminist variant, the Deity takes that role. Is this a slip on the part of Narguiss's father? Possibly but not necessarily. The reversal renders the Arabic text less difficult to comprehend. The actor in both parts of the sentence is the

Deity—He receives the words and He forgives Adam. In the Koranic original, Adam receives the words and the Deity forgives him. Narguiss's mother, we assume, finds the message clearer.

The father is instilling a message in the mother (and in the reader). The Arabic reader of El Saadawi's text need not be told that the Koran is considered by believing Muslims to be the direct and unmediated word of God, perfect in every respect including language. Hence, when the father declares, "God had a deep knowledge of language and its rules. He would never use the singular or the dual except in the right context" (117), he is justifying the fact that, on a most literal level, Eve was not forgiven. For this contemporary Arab textual male, the issue is, therefore, quite clear-cut. The female remains outside the purview of the divine action. In this, Narguiss's father differs from many premodern commentators (for example, al-Tabarî, al-Qurtubî).[32]

The debate over who is and who is not forgiven by the Deity in the Muslim Holy Book is not the domain of only the premodern commentators, however. By raising this question, Nawal El Saadawi has again inserted her novel into a contemporary debate. One of the most popular genres in Islamist discourse today is the legal injunction, the *fatwâ*. A sort of religious "Dear Abby" column, the *fatwâ* involves a question posed to a religious authority who then provides an answer based on Islamic law and theology. A contemporary questioner from Abu Dhabi asks why it is that he did not read in the Koran a single verse that would indicate Eve's forgiveness, whereas Adam was forgiven, after the Deity received certain words from him. The complex answer provided by the religious authority boils down to the fact that Eve is forgiven along with Adam, an answer that would certainly not surprise some of the medieval commentators.[33]

The Saadawian discourse in *Jannât wa-Iblîs* is not so reassuring. The religious texts are stacked against the female. Yet this childhood brainwashing does not seem to have permanently affected either of the two leading female characters; they will both be destroyed, and together at that, but not before putting up a fight. Narguiss courageously confronts the Director, affirming her onomastic and sexual identity and walking away from the male political structure of which she has been a part for thirty years. The case of Ganat is more complicated. A rebel from the minute she was born, she had come out of her mother's belly with her eyes open, when all other children were born with theirs closed. Her grandmother spat on seeing this, and asked for God's forgiveness, wondering whether the creature was human or a jinn.

Ganat embodies the eternal woman, doomed to destruction. The color of her eyes is yellow, like that of a serpent's eyes, her nose is like that of the Sphinx, her skin is black like Eblis's. Women and the Devil are brought together in a combination familiar to readers of El Saadawi.[34]

Ganat's relationship to Eblis, then, is more than mere placement in the book title. As children, they loved one another and she even wrote him a poem.

> —I love you
>   Because you are the only one amongst the slaves
>   Who refused to kneel
>   Who said no. (216)

Ganat's admiration here is a reference to the Koranic verses in which Eblis, unlike all the angels, refuses God's order to bow down before Adam.[35]

Nawal El Saadawi's radical feminist vision not only is imbued with mainstream Arabo-Islamic religiolegal texts but comes close to a view of Eblis prevalent in Islamic mystical traditions. There he is excused, becoming a misunderstood victim. His refusal to bow before Adam, though an act of disobedience, is redefined. It represents a declaration of monotheism, and his resulting martyrdom is a necessary part of the divine plan.[36]

Ganat does not, however, have a monopoly on Eblis. He interacts with all the characters who populate the asylum. He is Nefissa's brother, and he is blamed for the illicit relationship between Ganat and

Narguiss. Eblis's most important act is, of course, the one he performs with the Deity. The two of them exist in a perennial tug-of-war in the Arabo-Islamic unconscious, signified by the popular phrase, "A'ûdhu bil-Lâh min al-Shaytân al-Rajîm" (I seek God's protection from Satan, the Damned).

Eblis is the scapegoat par excellence. In a sense, it is the Deity who urges him to unsavory acts. This vision of Eblis as an innocent victim of the patriarchal religious structure is not entirely new in contemporary Arabic bellelettristic texts. The twentieth-century male writer Tawfîq al-Hakîm (d. 1987) posed the problem in a 1954 short story entitled "The Martyr," which may also owe some inspiration to Sufi traditions.[37]

In Tawfîq al-Hakîm's text, the Devil wishes to repent and change his ways. At Christmas, he descends on the Vatican and requests an audience with the pope. He expresses his desire to enter the "haven of faith," to which the pope reacts in confusion. But the Devil is not to be swayed. He repeats his request and pleads with the pontiff to save him. The pope refuses this appeal. The Devil is sent away, but not before being advised to turn to the other religions. This he does, going next to the grand rabbi. This religious authority realizes that "Satan's finding of faith would make the structure of Jewish privilege collapse, and destroy the glory of the sons of Israel."[38] The grand rabbi comes to the same conclusion as his Christian counterpart, but with the stated reason that Judaism does not "conduct missionary work."[39] Then Satan turns to the shaykh al-azhar, head of the international Muslim citadel of traditional learning. Like his earlier colleagues, the shaykh ponders the question, but Satan receives the same treatment he had met with earlier. The Devil's last recourse is the Angel Gabriel at the gate of Paradise. Not surprisingly, the Devil is turned away by Gabriel, as he was by the earthly religious authorities.

The Satan of Tawfîq al-Hakîm is, like his Saadawian manifestation, embroiled with the three monotheistic religions, and like his literary cousin, he is a victim. But his victimization does not come about through a direct encounter with the Deity, as it does in *The Innocence of the Devil*. The shaykh al-azhar realizes the importance of the duo when he wonders about the effect of the phrase "I seek God's protection from Satan, the Damned." In al-Hakîm's vision, the Devil is doomed to exist eternally in this relationship with the Deity. Not so in El Saadawi's narrative, where both the incarcerated Deity and the Devil are destroyed. No eternal life can be had for either of them. Their destruction means the destruction of the patriarchal system from which they emanate.

El Saadawi has gone a step beyond her male compatriot. She has redefined the monotheistic struggle between God and the Devil and added a feminist twist to the encounter. Her narrative is complicated not only by other characters but also by the serpent, which has been there all along—physically in a crack in the wall as well as in the imagery evoked by the text.

Adam and Eve. Eblis and the serpent. A novel whose Arabic title, *Jannât wa-Iblîs,* evokes all these elements and offers a clue that our subject is the Garden of Eden. Is this to say that the insane asylum is the Garden of Eden? On a certain level, yes: this is where the serpent pops up its head, where we find Eblis hiding behind a tree, where the Deity walks around. Yet the signals that the narrator sends us about this locus are subtle. When Nefissa's brother dies, his mother is told that he is in the Garden of Eden. When Nefissa searches for her brother in Cairo, a man on the street tells her to look for him either in prison or in the insane asylum. Is this brother Eblis? That is what we are led to believe. If so, then he is in the insane asylum. Or is it the Garden of Eden?

To say that the asylum functions on one level as the literary metaphorical universe that evokes the Garden of Eden is really tantamount to saying that the Adam and Eve story functions as one of the subtexts for Nawal El Saadawi's *Jannât wa-Iblîs.* Unlike the Garden of Eden that conjures up a specific historical moment, however, El Saadawi's literary creation does the opposite. Its historical framework is precisely the antithesis of a specific moment: it speaks to the universality and everlasting nature of the religious and cultural paradigms it seeks to uncover.

ENDNOTES

[1] Nawâl al-Sa'dâwî, *Jannât wa-Iblîs* (Beirut: Dâr al-Adâb, 1992). I follow the transcriptions and translations in the English text, except for the correction of evident mistakes, which are noted.

[2] For an in-depth study of this novel and other works of El Saadawi, see Fedwa Malti-Douglas, *Men, Women, and God(s): Nawal El Saadawi and Arab Feminist Poetics* (Berkeley and Los Angeles: University of California Press, forthcoming).

[3] Nawal El Saadawi, "An Overview of My Life," trans. Antoinette Tuma, in *Contemporary Authors Autobiography Series*, vol. 11, ed. Mark Zadrozny (Detroit: Gale Research, 1990); Allen Douglas and Fedwa Malti-Douglas, "Reflections of a Feminist: Conversation with Nawal al-Saadawi," in *Opening the Gates: A Century of Arab Feminist Writing*, ed. Margot Badran and Miriam Cooke (London and Bloomington: Virago and Indiana University Press, 1990); Nawal El Saadawi, personal communication, February 15, 1994. For the works on sexuality and gender, see Nawâl al-Sa'dâwî: *al-Mar'a wal-Jins*, 3d ed. (Cairo: Maktabat Madbûlî, 1974); *al-Unthâ Hiya al-Asl* (Cairo: Maktabat Madbûlî, 1974); *al-Rajul wal-Jins* (Beirut: al-Mu'assasa al-'Arabiyya lil-Dirâsât wal-Nashr, 1976); and *al-Mar'a wal-Sirâ' al-Nafsî* (Cairo: Maktabat Madbûlî, 1983).

[4] Nawâl al-Sa'dâwî, *Suqût al-Imâm* (Cairo: Dâr al-Mus-

taqbal al-'Arabî, 1987), trans. Sherif Hetata as *The Fall of the Imam* (London: Methuen, 1988). See Malti-Douglas, *Men, Women, and God(s)*, chap. 5, for a discussion of this novel.

5 Nawal El Saadawi discusses the association in her introduction to *Women of the Arab World: The Coming Challenge*, ed. Nahid Toubia, trans. Nahed El Gamal (London: Zed Books, 1988), 1–7. The volume is comprised of papers presented at an AWSA conference in Cairo.

6 I am grateful to Nawal El Saadawi for many of these biographical details.

7 Nawâl al-Sa'dâwî, *Ma'raka Jadîda fî Qadiyyat al-Mar'a* (Cairo: Sînâ lil-Nashr, 1992).

8 Douglas and Malti-Douglas, "Reflections," 399.

9 Nawâl al-Sa'dâwî; *Mudhakkirât Tifla Ismuhâ Su'âd* (Cairo: Manshûrât Dâr Tadâmun al-Mar'a al-'Arabiyya, 1990).

10 Nawâl al-Sa'dâwî, *al-Hubb fî Zaman al-Naft* (Cairo: Maktabat Madbûlî, 1993).

11 Nawal El Saadawi, *The Hidden Face of Eve: Women in the Arab World*, trans. Sherif Hetata (Boston: Beacon Press, 1982).

12 Nawâl al-Sa'dâwî, *Mudhakkirât Tabîba* (Beirut: Dâr al-Adâb, 1980). The first chapter has been translated by Fedwa Malti-Douglas as "Growing Up Female in Egypt," in *Women and the Family in the Middle East: New Voices of Change*, ed. Elizabeth Warnock Fernea (Austin: University of Texas Press, 1985), 111–20. The entire text has been translated as Nawal El Saadawi, *Memoirs of a Woman Doctor*, trans. Catherine Cobham (San Francisco: City Lights Books, 1989). I have discussed the issues of censorship and religion with El Saadawi on many occasions.

¹³ Nawal El Saadawi, personal communication, April 14, 1993.

¹⁴ See, for example, Muhammad Fu'âd 'Abd al-Bâqî, *al-Mu'jam al-Mufahras li-Alfâz al-Qur'ân al-Karîm* (Beirut: Mu'assasat Jamâl lil-Nashr, n.d.), 180–82.

¹⁵ See, for example, Jalâl al-Dîn al-Mahallî and Jalâl al-Dîn al-Suyûtî, *Tafsîr al-Qur'ân* (Cairo: Mustafâ al-Bâbî al-Halabî, 1966), vol. 2, 251–52; al-Tabarî, *Tafsîr al-Tabarî— Jâmi' al-Bayân fî Ta'wîl al-Qur'ân* (Beirut: Dâr al-Kutub al-'Ilmiyya, 1992), vol. 11, 313–14; al-Baydâwî, *Tafsîr al-Baydâwî* (Beirut: Dâr al-Kutub al-'Ilmiyya, 1988), vol. 2, 402–3.

¹⁶ For a list of these verses, see 'Abd al-Bâqî, *al-Mu'jam*, 182.

¹⁷ *Al-Qur'ân*, Sûrat al-Najm, verses 19, 20, 27.

¹⁸ See, for example, W. Montgomery Watt, *Islamic Philosophy and Theology* (Edinburgh: Edinburgh University Press, 1962), 58–81.

¹⁹ See Malti-Douglas, *Men, Women, and God(s)*, which discusses the other referential universes associated with rape of the female.

²⁰ For a discussion of this association, see Fedwa Malti-Douglas, *Woman's Body, Woman's Word: Gender and Discourse in Arabo-Islamic Writing* (Princeton: Princeton University Press, 1991), 48–49, 59.

²¹ See, for example, Samîra 'Itânî, *Hal Sahîh anna Akthar Ahl al-Nâr Hum al-Nisâ'?* (Beirut: Dâr al-Fath lil-Tibâ'a wal-Nashr, 1979[?]); 'A'id ibn 'Abd Allâh al-Qarnî, *Makâ'id al-Shaytân* (Riyad: Dâr al-Diyâ' lil-Nashr wal-Tawzî', 1411 A.H.); 'A'id ibn 'Abd Allâh al-Qarnî, *Bâqat Ward ilâ Fatât al-Islâm* (Riyad: Dâr al-Diyâ' lil-Nashr wal-Tawzî', 1411 A.H.), 29.

[22] See, for example, John L. Esposito, *Islam: The Straight Path* (New York: Oxford University Press, 1991), 14.

[23] This is not the first verse of the Koran; the translation is in error. The Arabic original makes no reference to the location of the verse.

[24] The translation gives "Lot's mother," though the correct translation is "Lot's people."

[25] *Al-Qur'ân,* Sûrat al-A'râf, verses 80–81; A. J. Arberry, *The Koran Interpreted* (New York: Macmillan, 1974), vol. 1, 181.

[26] See Charles Pellat, "Liwât," in *Sexuality and Eroticism among Males in Moslem Societies,* ed. Arno Schmitt and Jehoeda Sofer (New York: Harrington Park Press, 1992), 152.

[27] See, for example, Everett K. Rowson, "The Categorization of Gender and Sexual Irregularity in Medieval Arabic Vice Lists," in *Body Guards: The Cultural Politics of Gender Ambiguity,* ed. Julia Epstein and Kristina Straub (New York: Routledge, 1991), 50–79; Everett K. Rowson, "The Effeminates of Early Medina," *Journal of the American Oriental Society* 111 (1992): 671–93. See also the various studies in *Sexuality and Eroticism,* ed. Schmitt and Sofer.

[28] See 'Abd al-Bâqî, *al-Mu'jam.*

[29] For the Koranic story, see *al-Qur'ân,* Sûrat al-Baqara, verses 35–38; Sûrat al-A'râf, verses 19–23; Sûrat Tâhâ, verses 120–21. See also John A. Phillips, *Eve: The History of an Idea* (San Francisco: Harper and Row, 1984), 148–55; Malti-Douglas, *Woman's Body, Woman's Word,* 45–46.

[30] See, for example, Ibn al-Batanûnî, *Kitâb al-'Unwân fî Makâyid al-Niswân,* MS., Cairo, Adâb 3568. For a discussion of Ibn al-Batanûnî's misogynist vision, see Malti-Douglas, *Woman's Body, Woman's Word,* 54–66.

[31] *Al-Qur'ân,* Sûrat al-Baqara, verse 37; Arberry, *Koran Interpreted,* vol. 1, 34.

[32] For an in-depth discussion of this material, see Malti-Douglas, *Men, Women, and God(s),* chap. 6.

[33] Mûsâ Sâlih Sharaf, *Fatâwâ al-Nisâ' al-'Asriyya* (Beirut and Cairo: Dâr al-Jîl and Maktabat al-Turâth al-Islâmî, 1988), 100.

[34] See Malti-Douglas, *Men, Women, and God(s),* chap. 5.

[35] See 'Abd al-Bâqî, *al-Mu'jam,* 134, 344.

[36] Peter J. Awn, *Satan's Tragedy and Redemption: Iblîs in Sufi Psychology* (Leiden: E. J. Brill, 1983). Neil Forsyth's *The Old Enemy: Satan and the Combat Myth* (Princeton: Princeton University Press, 1987), omits the Islamic Satan and Adam and Eve story.

[37] Tawfîq al-Hakîm, "The Martyr," trans. David Bishai, rev. Ronald Ewart, in *Arabic Writing Today: The Short Story,* ed. Mahmoud Manzalaoui (Cairo: Dar al-Maaref, 1968), 36–46.

[38] Ibid., 40.

[39] Ibid., 41.

1 *Ganat Arrives*

That morning the sun pierced through the clouds that
had gathered during the night. Then the huge gate
opened. Its iron hinges made a screeching noise like
an ancient water wheel. In the deep silence the noise
was sudden, unexpected. The birds flew up, making
sounds like twittering.

There were figures squatting on the ground. They
were human, men and women. Their eyes, half-closed
as though in sleep, opened wide. The ground on which
they were squatting was hard, covered in sand with
drying grass and thorny plants. It was the kind of veg-
etation which grows wild, seemingly without water or
sustenance of any kind – cultivated by the Devil, as people
say. The sky over their heads was a huge grey-coloured
expanse thick with dust. There was no movement, no
breeze. The air was heavy with smoke and defeat.

The men were gathered in their usual place, dressed
in wide *gallabeyas*[1] which were all white, like the colour

[1] A long robe almost like a nightshirt.

of sickness. At each waist was a thin belt. According to the official records their belts had a special significance. They indicated affliction with a chronic disease like tuberculosis or leprosy. If one of them so much as looked into the eyes of someone else the malady was instantly transmitted. They stared fixedly into space with half-open eyes and their gaze reflected a total awareness of death. Over their surfaces floated a film of tears which neither dried completely nor dropped off. The hair on their heads had been shaven to conform with the instructions issued by the Director. Their faces were covered with sparse scraggy beards which straggled down over their chests. No one could tell their age.

They resembled one another. All but one man. They called him Eblis.[1] He was young and clean-shaven, without beard or whiskers, and his hair had rebelled against the law. It was long, and in front a lock blew freely in the wind, sometimes dropping down over his forehead. He lifted it up with a finger. In the daytime his eyes were black. Sometimes they would flash with a beam of light as though he had been touched with a sudden feverish madness. Then the beam of light in them would disappear, revealing a tear full of sadness.

The walls were high, and along them, at the top, ran a barbed wire fence. The heads of the trees bent in the wind with a heavy, slow movement.

[1] Satan or the Devil.

Eblis's eyes circled round and stopped at the big iron gate.

The women were confined to a special area. It was called the *harim's*[1] corner. They squatted on the ground with their heads wrapped in white veils as though just back from a pilgrimage to Mecca, their arms always folded over their breasts. They leaned a cheek on one hand and kept their lips tightly closed.

The silence was broken by the noise of the big iron gate opening. The iron posts on either side shook, and the walls of the Yellow Palace [2] trembled as it clanged wide open.

The Yellow Palace was also called the House, a word which by itself had no special significance. It evoked nothing in the mind unless it was preceded by another word composed of only three letters: *mad*. It had been an old palace built in the days of the Pharaohs. A King had lived in it. He thought that the heavens and the earth, that men and women were his property, that he owned them. Then he died, just as horses die. They buried him in the earth together with his horse, and his sword. After that all that remained of him was a small piece of iron in the shape of a U. It was the horseshoe which had been nailed to the hoof of his

---

[1] That which is forbidden. Originates from *haram* which means not allowed in religion; contrary to the code of behaviour, sinful, punishable.
[2] Popular term for madhouse.

horse. They kept it in a glass cubicle in the city museum so that tourists could visit it.

The walls of the palace had started to crumble centuries ago. Many palaces had collapsed before and were no more. But not this palace. It was said by the people that the Devil lived in it, and kept it from falling. The Devil was mad. He did not believe in such things as time, or God, or the Director, or the Head Nurse.

The iron gate opened. Dust rose into the air. A brigade of policemen stamped over the ground on their iron heels like horses on their hooves. Their brass helmets shone with a red glare. They were followed by a group of male nurses wearing white aprons. The nurses' shoes were made of rubber and moved over the ground silently, but their breathing was loud. It kept going in and out with a panting sound through their wide-open mouths.

The moment she stepped in through the gate everything came to a halt. Even the birds ceased their twittering. They stood still on the barbed wire and watched the newcomer walk in. Their eyes shone like small dark beads.

Her body entered through the open gate with a movement which was unusual for a woman. She seemed to break in with her tall body, to throw herself through it, taut as an arrow, as though diving into the sea.

The eyes of the men and the women swung towards her. They looked into her eyes. They were eyes wide open to the world, like windows. They did not peer or blink, and the lashes curled up rebelliously as though ready to fight at any moment. Her pupils were black, steady, unmoving. Her hair was thick and dark, and the wind kept blowing it over her face. She threw it backwards every now and then with a movement which resembled a horse tossing its head. She walked barefoot and carried her shoes in her hand. They were made of black leather and had no heels, like the shoes of a dancer or an acrobat.

She charged through the black iron gate like a white arrow splitting the universe. Behind her ran a group of male nurses trying to catch up with her. One of them tried to get a hold on her arm, but she slipped out of his grasp. Another went for her other arm. She beat him off with her shoe.

No one had ever witnessed a scene like this in the palace, either in the early days, or more recently. People said it had taken thirty years to build. Slaves had carried the stones on their backs from the Mokattam Hills. They had climbed up the scaffolding slowly, whiplashes stinging their backs. It was said that they were the same slaves who had built the Pyramids of Khoufou[1] and Mankara'a.[2] But no one really knew the history of things before The Book.[3]

When The Book was mentioned on its own like that

[1] Cheops
[2] Menkane or Mycerinus.
[3] In Arabic *The Book* is the Holy Book, that is the Koran.

people understood. No other word was needed to explain which one was meant. It rang in the air and everyone knew that it referred to the Book of God. It was the only book allowed into the palace. No other book could ever find its way in. These were the instructions of the Director, and at night the Head Nurse inspected the wards. Her fingers dug into the cupboards and the drawers. She turned over the clothes inside them. The men hid books and love stories beneath their underwear. The women were more careful. The Head Nurse never found anything hidden in their underwear, except sometimes a small bloodstain, or the faint odour of an old dream long dead.

The eyes of the women could be perceived wide open and staring as they looked out through the glass partition which separated them off behind it. It was the first time they had seen a woman enter through the gate holding her body like that. Their necks stretched up with a movement which carried a hint of pride in it. Pride was contagious, and pride, even if only in one of their kind, was enough to spread the contagion. One of the women unfolded her arms from over her chest and stood up. She looked at her across the distance which separated them. Her mouth opened wide and a laugh escaped from between her lips. It rang out with joy and the other women squatting on the ground also started to laugh. Their bodies shook as they stifled their laughs so that no sound would be heard coming from them. The infection spread to the men. The stale air they held back in their chests burst out, not silently like the women, but with an audible sound. For the men were permitted to laugh, but not loudly. The only person who could laugh at the top of his voice without being punished was the Director. The Head Nurse too, if the Director was absent, or of course when she was alone in her room.

The scene that day was really unusual. Eblis was taking a walk. His eyes circled round the high wall several times, then stopped at the gate. After that they did not move. He lifted the lock of hair from over his forehead and looked at her as she walked in on her bare feet, carrying her shoes in her hand. Her eyes were wide open. They did not peer or blink. He felt he had seen her before. He was almost sure, but where? Her face, her features, the way she moved with pride, everything. Perhaps he had seen her in a dream or before he was born.

A laugh burst from his lips. His laugh was loud. He let it burst out, and after a while he was laughing uproariously, as though unable to hold it back. The infection spread to the other men, then to the women. The laughter burst out from their chests, and with it the air held back inside. It was loud, unrestrained. It rang in the air.

Warning sirens sounded all around. The Director's head looked out from the window of his office on the upper floor. Then the Head Nurse appeared, wearing a white veil around her head. She was leading a small force of male nurses who carried cane sticks in their hands. They pounced on the women and beat them on the buttocks with stinging strokes.

– All of you back to the wards. All of you back inside.

The women ran like chicks and stumbled quickly inside. All except one woman. She walked slowly, her eyes fixed on the newcomer. The features were new and yet strangely familiar. She had seen this defiant sweeping movement somewhere, like the movement of a wild mare, running free, not owned by anybody, never ridden before.

A male nurse rushed up to her and stung her over the buttocks with his cane.

– Make it quick, girl. Get a move on, Nefissa.

She idled, swinging her buttocks disdainfully as she walked. The cane came down on them again. She turned on him angrily.

– Showing off with the women. Why don't you beat the men?

– Inside quickly, girl. The Director is coming.

The male nurses never beat the men on their buttocks. They confined themselves to an angry exclamation, or a prod in the shoulder with the cane.

Soon they were all back in the wards. All except Eblis. He hid behind the trunk of a tree. With him was another man, elderly, with a long white beard and a turban wound round his head. It was shaped like a cone with a pointed tip. At the top was a black feather rising in the air like a cockscomb. The male nurse prodded him in the shoulder with his cane.

– Come on, quickly. Can't you see the Director's here?

– Director, my foot, you ass. Don't you know who I am?

– I know, Your Holiness, I know. But get inside quickly. Let my day end in peace.

The Director was standing at the main entrance to the palace. His body was hidden inside the folds of his white coat. The Chief of the police force stood in front of him. He held a sheet of paper folded in the form of a cone. He handed it to the Director.

– This is for you, sir. You have to sign for this woman.

The Director unfolded the paper. He stared at it for a moment. His eyes shifted from the paper in his hand to the woman standing holding her shoes in one hand. Her eyes circled around, taking in her new surroundings. She smiled. He pulled out his pen from his breast pocket and scrawled his signature on the paper. The Chief of the police force gave the woman a parting look, then saluted, clicking his heels and stamping his foot on the ground several times, before turning his back on the Director and marching out of the iron gate at the head of his force. His men stamped their heels on the ground like horses as they followed behind.

The Head Nurse was standing behind the Director. Around her neck hung a thread, or a thin chain. It carried a whistle. It looked like a small mouse hiding in a furrow between her breasts. Her head, wrapped in the white veil, was bent to the ground and her eyes stole quick glances at the bare feet of the woman standing in front of them, then climbed up her legs. The muscles of her legs were taut inside a pair of narrow leather trousers. Around her waist she wore a wide belt. Her shirt was white and cut very wide. It floated around her body and her long, dark neck emerged from it like a tree-trunk rising from the earth. Her eyes were wide open, with a staring look which hinted at some madness.

– What's your name?

– Ganat.

Her mouth opened wide as she pronounced her name. Then she smiled. Her face lit up. Her love for her name was an old love. It had started long ago. Ganat was the plural of *Gana*.[1] That was what her father had said to her.

Her eyes started to circle round again. They stopped at the Head Nurse. She stared steadily into her eyes for a long moment, as though trying to remember.

– Narguiss?

[1] Heaven or Paradise.

The Head Nurse gave a nervous shake of her veiled head as though refuting something.

– I am the Head Nurse.

She lifted her hand to the whistle lying at her breast and twirled the long chain with her finger like a rosary. It circled round and round. Her lips muttered a verse to chase away the evil spirits.

The voice of the Director rang out in the big compound, moving down between the stone columns into the open spaces.

– Solitary confinement under supervision, and three sessions a week.

– I shall see to it, sir.

The voice of the Head Nurse seemed to emerge from between clenched teeth. There was no movement of her lips. Then everybody disappeared, leaving four male nurses and Ganat standing with her shoes in her hand. She thought she would go up to her room alone, but eight arms reached out to take her away. They marched her through long dark corridors, climbed one floor after another, up crumbling steps that complained under their feet and let out choking sounds like dying cats. They put her in a room adjoining the female ward and locked the door on her. She heard the key screeching in the lock. It pierced her ears as she lay on the bed with her eyes closed.

It was like an old dream that was suddenly becoming real. She opened her lids, then closed them again.

Where was she? This window with iron bars, she had seen it before, in her sleep, in another life before she was born.

She opened her eyes and looked out through the iron bars. She could see a never-ending desert, expanse after expanse of sand. She moved the look of her eyes closer to where she lay, followed the high stone wall down to an open space of bare ground surrounding the palace. They called it the garden. There was nothing but dying grass distributed in patches and a stone column with Pharaonic inscriptions engraved on it. She had seen these designs before. They had the same form as the Ibis calf and the god Ra'a[1] whom she had read about in her school books. It was during the first year of preparatory school and the gods had horns on their heads.

She spotted him hiding behind a tree-trunk. He was wearing a white *gallabeya*. It hung loose around his body, gathered up by a narrow belt at the waist. His hair was black and thick and it covered the back of his neck. A male nurse kept circling around the tree-trunk trying to catch him. He dodged away from him, clapping his hands in glee, like a child playing hide-and-seek.

– Here I am, here I am.

He lifted his face, saw her standing at the window.

[1] The god of the sun.

Their eyes met in a long look as though they had known one another before. She called out.

– I am Ganat.

Her voice rang out, then gradually died away across the open spaces. He stood without movement, his eyes staring at the window. Her name was Ganat, and here he was dreaming of just one *Gana*.

The male nurse pounced on him and grasped him by the arm.

– I've caught you, Eblis.

The name rang in her ears. Could it be him? Could it?

2 *The First Session*

She half-opened her eyelids and peered through them
furtively into the dark. It was as though she were hiding
from herself as she tried to steal a look at the world.
The ceiling looked drab. It was cracked, with patches
of moisture which had seeped through a long time ago.
Perhaps it was rain from the time of Noah's Ark. The
wooden rafters were old and wormeaten, bending
under the weight of the years. The bed creaked beneath
her the way it used to do when she slept in her
grandmother's room.

Her eyes grew wider and blacker with surprise. Where
was the white, plastic-coated ceiling? And the fine blue
curtain? The black of her eyes looked even more black
in the two circles of pure white which surrounded
them. She moved her look over the surface of the
cracked walls. The humidity and cold of winter alternates
with the heat of summer. The moisture dries, then the
coat of plaster cracks. Patches fall off haphazardly or
in a pattern. A universal order, meticulously exact,

leaving nothing to chance. This she knew from her grandfather. How else could the patches which had fallen off have left the form of the god Ra'a and the Ibis calf? Its horns curved forwards in a movement which was visible and its eyes bulged like the eyes of Sheikh[1] Bassiouni.

Sheikh Bassiouni.

She rubbed her eyes with her finger. It was grey, the colour of old granite. It had remained hidden from every ray of sun since her son had died. Perhaps it was the finger of another woman, and this other woman had lived and died only to come to life again and rub her half-open lids with the tip of her grey finger.

She stretched her finger. Its greyness protruded from a thin, emaciated hand. Her arm was like a thin cane stick in the folds of the white sleeve. The sleeve ended in flounces around the wrist, and the wrist was surrounded with big bangles. She wondered where her wrist-watch could have gone.

The five fingers of her hand crept over the cracked marble top. Their shadow moved over the wall. They resembled the fingers of her grandmother. She picked up the small wrist-watch. It was a golden disc and her mother had given it to her as a present when she passed her final preparatory stage examinations. She moved the small dial close up to her eyes. It was the size of a *piastre*[2]

[1] A religious dignitary.
[2] A coin equivalent to one hundredth of an Egyptian pound.

or a copper *millime*.[1] The dial almost touched her eyelids.

She could not see the hands, and the numbers on the dial looked like black circles with jagged tails, like the legs of a fly swimming in water.

Her body shivered on the bed. She could hear the twang of the wires under the mattress. At one time she was able to see the small hand of the dial in pitch dark. Then it started to be invisible when she tried to see it in the night without a light. Now the big hand was growing invisible too. Was it a sign of approaching death? Was she witnessing a withdrawal of the spirit from her body? Her eyes opened wide. Now she was remembering what she had forgotten a while ago. She could no longer see things, see the world as it really was without wearing her spectacles.

She stretched out her hand to her spectacles, put them on her nose and settled the frame in place. She did not look at the watch. She realised that she had no need to know what time it was. She pushed the bridge of her spectacles away from her nose with a quick movement of her hand. It took less than the fraction of a second. But to the Director this was a sign that she had lost her sanity.

He was sitting next to her bed. He stared at her. His grey eyes looked out from behind the glass of his spectacles. The Head Nurse stood beside him clothed in her white uniform. She held a syringe in her hand.

[1] A coin equivalent to one thousandth of an Egyptian pound.

The shadow of the needle was like a long, thin blade on the wall. She plunged the needle under the sleeve into her arm, pulled it out, then rubbed the spot with a small piece of cotton moistened with alcohol.

The smell of alcohol shot up her nose. It reminded her of school, of the nurses' room. The fingers of the Head Nurse were long and pale, and they trembled. She kept her eyes on the ceiling and avoided looking at her. The Head Nurse rubbed her arm with the piece of cotton several times to stop the bleeding, but one red spot remained visible on the white sleeve of her nightshirt.

Ever since she was a child the sight of blood had scared her. Was it really fear? Perhaps it was something else, something nearer to joy. Or curiosity. Like a criminal desire to know about things, which made her want to pluck the forbidden fruit. When her grandmother slaughtered a chicken she would gaze at the dark red colour of the blood, as though it were her blood that she saw.

She looked up. She wanted to see the eyes of the Director as they stared out through the glass of his spectacles, but he was gone. The Head Nurse had gone too. There was no one. Above in the drab ceiling a pair of eyes looked out at her from a crack. She could see them examining her with a fixed stare. The head was like that of a small, serpent-like creature, and the tail was thin and long and curled forwards like the horns of the Ibis calf.

The surprise caught her unawares, and the watch dropped out of her hand on to the floor making a sharp noise. The small serpent laughed and disappeared into the crack. But its laughter sounded like the sobs of a weeping child.

– Heh, heh, heh, heh.

The sound reminded her of her mother when she wept at night. Her weeping echoed in her ears like the whistling of a distant wind. Her mother stood at the window. She had a high forehead and a straight nose. Her nose was lifted proudly up. Her cheek bones were sharply defined, and her eyes were charcoal black. A thin thread of blood trickled down from the corner of her mouth.

Ganat hid her head under the pillow. The image of her mother invaded her from all sides. An avalanche of images poured down on her head like cold water. The cold of the water reacted with the feverish heat in her head. Beads of sweat stood out on her brow. Steam rose from her nostrils and its pressure made everything shake: the sheets, the mattress, and the four legs of the bed.

She lifted her hands out from under the sheet, grasped the edge of the sheet, wound it round her body and held on to it for dear life, as though she were desperately trying to prevent her life from slipping from her body.

– Ganat?

She strained, her ears sensitive to the sound of her

name. Was it her name? It was as though she were hearing it for the first time. Perhaps she had heard it before, called out by her grandfather, or her father. He used to say that Ganat was the plural of *Gana*. She asked him what *Gana* meant, so he opened the book and read:

– The *Gana* of Eden in which flow rivers of honey and milk.

She did not like the taste of honey, nor that of milk, and preferred salted cheese or pickles.

She opened her eyes, stole a look around her. The ceiling was grubby and showed cracks. The plaster had fallen leaving the image of the Ibis calf showing on it. Where was the ceiling covered in a clean white coat of paint? Where was the fine blue curtain? And the wide bed with Zakaria's face looking out from it?

– Zakaria?

Was it her voice calling out to him? It was as though she were hearing his name for the first time. Zakaria? The name sounded strange to her and yet at the same time it was familiar. She had heard it repeated so often in her life, and yet whenever she heard it, it was as though she were hearing it for the first time. Her picture hung in a golden frame on the smooth white wall. Beside her was a man dressed in a black tailcoat, the kind bridegrooms wore. On his upper lip he had a black moustache, and wound around his neck was a broad ribbon tied in a bow. Her mother called it a *papillon,*[1] and would look at Ganat standing beside him in her wedding dress. The dress was white, the same colour as the shroud used to wrap a body inside a coffin. In her arms she held a bouquet of roses. One rose in the middle hung down. It was so pale. It looked as though it had not a single drop of blood in it. The bed was made of chestnut wood, and was big, big enough for death to lie in it.

His face stood out over the edge of the sheet and had the same white pallor as the sheet. It was a strange face. It was as though she had never seen it before, and yet she felt that she had seen it many times. In fact, she had seen it every day; every day for over thirty years. But now it had grown longer, and his hair had fallen off his head. Only a patch of hair above each ear was left. The patch was grey. His body inside the silk pyjamas was no longer firm and taut. Its muscles had grown flabby. The black iris of his eye was drowning in a blue-white sea, and the blue-white sea was turning yellow with each passing hour.

His lips opened and let out a croak.

– Ganat.

It resembled the voice of her grandfather when he called out to her. He sat in his study behind a desk coated and polished in ebony black. His face reflected itself in its glass top. His nose was big and hooked. It

[1] French for bow-tie. Also butterfly. At the time of the King, French was often spoken by the aristocracy and those who imitated them, as a second language instead of English.

proved his descent from the noble line of his father and his grandfather whose memory was cherished by all. No one in the family had ever been born without that nose. It looked like the beak of a duck. All of them had been born with it, except for one child to whom her mother's aunt had given birth many years ago. This child had a small nose, not a big hooked one. No one ever found out what happened to it after it was born. The mother drowned herself in the waters of the Nile at dawn.

At night she cuddled up close to her grandmother in the big brass four-poster bed. She could hear her grandfather clear his throat as he sat in his study. He hemmed and hawed in a hoarse voice as though emphasising the fact that he was the male of the house, and that he was still alive, or that he was wide awake to what was happening around him.

In the silence of the night she would slip out of bed and walk across the hall. The door of the study was ajar. She could see her grandfather sitting in a chair reading.

She whispered in her grandmother's ear.

– What is Grandfather writing, Nena?[1]

Her grandmother opened her toothless mouth and yawned.

– Nothing but nonsense. That's what he writes, she would say.

[1] A diminutive, endearing term for Grandmother.

In the morning she crept into his study. The shelves of the library hung high above her head. She stood on a chair, stretched her body upwards as far as she could, lifting herself on her toes, and pulled out a book with a smooth glossy cover. The words were written in golden letters. She caressed the fine, silky pages, then tore one out and folded it to make a winged paper dart.

Her grandfather came in and caught her doing this. He pulled the book out of her hands, shouting at the top of his voice.

– It's the Book of God, you stupid little ass.

He thrashed her with his cane before she went to bed. She lay next to her grandmother stifling her sobs, and the posts of the bed shook with her sobbing. She did not know that God wrote books like her grandfather did.

– Nena, does God know how to write like Grandfather does? she asked.

– Of course. God is greater than your Grandfather. He is above us all.

She could not imagine that there was anyone above her grandfather except for the King. And the King did not write books. She had heard from her father that the King was corrupt, that he spent his nights drinking in the company of women who danced. But the library of her grandfather was full of books. Had her grandfather written all these books? It was a question she

asked herself when she grew a little older. Her grandmother later told her that he had written only two
books. After that he stopped writing and died. The
King sent them a telegram of condolences, and her
grandmother put a golden frame round it and hung it
on the wall. She pointed it out with her finger to everyone
who came to pay respects to the family of the deceased.
Every time she did that her eyes would light up. Ganat's
mother and father kept looking at the telegram hanging
on the wall and immediately their eyes would shine in
the same way. It was printed on paper with decorated
gilt edges.

At night as she lay in bed it dawned on her that the
happiness bestowed on her family by the King's telegram had been greater than the sadness caused by her
grandfather's death.

She felt her heart grow heavy with guilt. She too
was not sad at her grandfather's death. She was brim-
ming with happiness when the day ended and he did
not come home. Now she could spend her days in his
study without having to fear anything. She slept peace-
fully. There was only one question that kept going
round and round in her head.

How was it that her grandfather had written two
books whereas God had written only one?

In the study her eyes kept moving over the books.
They were looking for the book written by God. Her
father called it the Koran, and her hand caressed its

smooth leather binding. It had a peculiar smell that went up her nose. She thought it was the smell of God. Now it reminded her of the smell of her grandfather, of old books with their printed letters, of wooden shelves, and leather chairs, of the thick dusty carpet, of stagnant air in closed working rooms.

She peered through her half-open eyes stealing a furtive glance at the world as though hiding what she was doing from herself. The ceiling was grubby and showed cracks. The Head Nurse stood close to her bed dressed in her white uniform. Her head was clothed in a grey veil, and she had a syringe in her hand.

Ganat pulled her arm violently away.

— I don't want injections.

— You must have an injection.

— I'm not sick.

— You are sick.

— Sick with what?

— It's not necessary for you to know.

— I must know.

She hit the top of the table with her hand.

— I want to know.

She kicked the air with her legs, waved her arms wildly.

— I have to know.

— You don't have to know.

The voice of the Head Nurse sounded hoarse. It

reminded her of her grandfather. When he died her grandmother no longer had to fear him. She extracted the Bible from under her pillow and called it God's book. She made the sign of the cross over her breast. Our Father which art in Heaven, forgive us our trespasses. Her grandmother's father was a Copt[1] from Upper Egypt. He owned a big farm and had black slaves working on it. Her grandfather wanted to inherit the farm so he married her grandmother. She had to abide by the holy laws of God and His Prophet, and to adopt Islam. She wanted to be sure that she would inherit from him when he died. She had heard that he owned a farm in the Delta region but she did not know that the Khedive[2] had taken it as a loan to help pay his debts. The ruler of the land was to be trusted and nobody ever thought of asking him for a receipt. If doubt ever crept into the heart of the person he was sure to become a victim of God's wrath long before it vented itself on the Khedive. That was what the daily *Al-Ahram* and the weekly *Aboul-Houl* explained at the time. Ganat's grandmother believed that what was written in the newspapers was always right. Yet she died without ever inheriting anything. Her father was angry with her because of what had happened. He felt he had been cheated into marrying his daughter to this man whom he had thought rich.

[1] An Egyptian Christian from the Orthodox Church.
[2] The ruler of Egypt before it became a kingdom.

So he retaliated by depriving her of the inheritance she was supposed to get from him. After some years her husband abandoned her. She had reached the age of despair[1] and was no longer suitable for him, so he married a girl of fourteen and never slept with Ganat's grandmother again.

– Our Father which art in Heaven, forgive us our trespasses.

– What is the age of despair, Nena?

– You don't need to know that my child.

– I want to know, Nena.

– You don't have to, I said.

– I want to know. I want to know.

Ganat waved her little fist in the air. Her grandmother's face resembled that of the Head Nurse. It was full of wrinkles. Between her ashen-coloured lips she held a whistle. She blew the whistle and her cheeks ballooned with air. She pulled the whistle from her lips and ran away gleefully clapping her hands. The girls in class gathered round her and their laughter rang out.

– Ha, ha, ha, ha.

The Headmistress came out. She had a big hooked nose like her grandfather. Her head was covered in a white veil. Between her fingers she held a long, tapering pencil. The Head Nurse was wearing the face of the Headmistress. A long chain hung down between her

[1] The menopause.

breasts. It carried a whistle. She blew into the whistle and it emitted a long, drawn-out sound like a bugle. Immediately four male nurses wearing white aprons rushed into the room.

Ganat never stopped struggling except when she lost consciousness. Maybe it was the drug they injected into her. Or someone hit her over the head with an iron bar and she fell into a coma almost like death. Her skeleton seemed to become separate from her body, taking her flesh with it. Nothing remained behind except something like a single throbbing cell which clung to the inner surface of her scalp and continued to follow what was going on. She could tell they were taking her away on a wheeled trolley. Her hands and feet were tied with ropes. They pushed her down a long, dark corridor. She could hear the sounds of the wheels on the tiled floor. Through her eyelids she glimpsed a ceiling. It was grubby and cracked, and part of the plaster had fallen off leaving a strange shape which looked like the body of a man with the head of a goat, and a woman with the tail of a fish like a siren from the sea. Her head shook with the movement of the wheels over the floor. It hit against the door-frame as they passed through it. They laid her body down on a table. The table was cold and it was covered with a rubber sheet. They tied her body to the legs of the table with a rope, and put a square of rubber between her teeth. They tied a leather belt around her head. It had a long wire coming out of it which had a black plug fixed to it at the other end.

Suddenly her body contracted. Her arms and legs jerked and quivered, straining against the ropes. Although she was screaming no sound emerged from her mouth, but her teeth chattered and gave out loud clicks.

Then her body went limp. It ceased moving and her arms lay listlessly by her side. One arm gave a last jerk before it dropped down over the edge of the table. It hung down loosely beside her body, swaying slightly like a pendulum.

The Head Nurse extended her hand and took hold of her arm, then lifted it up alongside her body lying on the table. Her fingers crept down to the wrist. She felt the pulse.

– Dub, dub, dub, dub.

The beats under her ribs were vigorous. Their rhythm was regular, like an old dance handed down from ages past. The leaves of the trees danced in the wind and with them the ears of corn in the fields. The music wafted through the air to her ears. It was smooth and tender like her mother's voice singing to her as she rocked her in the cot.

– Hou, hou, sleep my sweet, sleep.

She opened her eyes. She could see her mother's face swathed in a white veil. Her eyes were black with a thin film of moisture. She caressed her on the shoulder and whispered in a voice she knew so well.

– Ganat.

3 *Another Woman*

The voice flowed into her ears like the whisper of a soft wind. It hovered over her eyelids like a feather, enveloping her in the warmth of her mother's voice as she rocked her cot gently, and sang to her before sleep.

– Hou, hou, sleep my sweet, sleep.

She would fall asleep as though slipping into a warm sea. She swam like a fish, then opened her wings and flew over the water. She flapped her wings like a butterfly under the sun; the sky was a clear blue. She ran over the grass with naked feet. The ears of corn danced in the wind. The smell of living green invaded her. She continued to run without stopping. Behind her she could hear his voice hunting her down, and words that hit her in the back like bullets.

– Fallen woman. Whore.

She fell flat on her face as she ran, felt the ground under the palm of her hand. Where was the wide bed? The fine curtain? And Zakaria?

Her hand reached out to him, moist with rain. The

skin on her other hand was dry and rough with swollen veins beneath the skin. It resembled her grandmother's hand. The beat of her heart under her ribs had the rhythm of the raindrops falling on the trees. The wind whistled in her ears with a sound like that of many voices shouting in unison.

– Down with the system! Down! Down!

She strained her ears. She longed to hear the voices shouting. Were they people shouting out loudly, or was she simply hearing things in her sleep. The voices faded into the silence. And the silence echoed in her ears like the roar of a million voices. They were all shouting, and they were all silent. The dark night enveloped them steadily. Nothing could stop it. The air was stagnant, heavy, loaded with the weight of defeat. Her face was turned to the window and her back to him.

– Fallen woman. Whore.

The words echoed in her ears with a familiar ring. It was as though she had heard them all her life. At school she used to hear Sheikh Bassiouni say:

– Fall, present. Fallen, past participle. She has fallen, third person, feminine.

She was a fallen woman like her mother Eve who fell into sin. She had a picture with the family. In it she was standing next to her mother. Her mother was sitting with her small sister on her knee. Her elder brother was standing near her father, his eyes half-closed. She stood at the edge of the picture. She was staring into the lens of the camera with a steady, wide-open look that had a hint of insanity in it.

What was it that she was seeing inside the lens of the camera? It could have been the eye of God, or maybe that of Satan. Perhaps it was just a vacuum, an emptiness which gathered around the focus of the lens in the form of a hole through which the whole world escaped into emptiness. Or maybe it was just the sun's rays falling on the lens, and reflecting themselves back into her eyes, so that she could not see anything at all.

She was born with her eyes wide open. People were born with their eyes closed. She came out of her mother's belly with an unblinking stare. Her grandmother spat into the opening of her bodice and said:

– I take refuge in Thee, o God, to protect us from Satan. Is this creature human, or is she a devil?

Men's eyes were attracted to her face. They lingered on her eyes. She had heard some of them say that her eyes had the brilliance and attraction of a great intelligence. However, such descriptions soon turned into an accusation. Others said there was a touch of madness in her. She was not normal. She was irresponsible, flighty.

The colour of her irises changed with the rotation of the earth. At night they were pitch black like the eyes of devils. During the day the sky was reflected in them and they became a clear blue like the eyes of angels. At dawn or at dusk her pupils had a red glare in them as though she were possessed by an evil spirit.

From the moment she learnt to read and write the letters of the alphabet she began to notice what men whispered into her ears. At school Sheikh Bassiouni said:

– Your eyes are full of the lust which is in Eve.

He pronounced the words in the classical language.[1] He taught language and religion. She did not know what the lust in Eve was. She asked her father. He gave her a look that made her hair stand up. One day as she was walking down the road a man whispered to her:

– You are a female.

His tongue hung out of his mouth after he had pronounced the word *female* as though he were gasping, and his eyes fastened themselves on her breasts with a look that meant she was a creature without brains who belonged to the mammalian species.

The way in which men described her eyes kept changing as she grew older. Some saw in them the deep sadness which was born ever since the day when Eve had sinned. Others saw innocence, a joy too vast to be contained by a whole world, and the chastity of the Virgin Mary. Some saw in them a great power of attraction, others a great power of repulsion. Some said that they were open without limit to the horizon;

[1] Not the spoken dialect.

others that they were closed, so closed they were impenetrable.

She was the only person who could not see her eyes except in the mirror. She was separated from them by a solid, shining barrier. She could see opaque, stony spheres like round pieces of marble. In the centre of each was a small dark opening like a bottomless pit.

– Fallen woman. Whore.

The voice resounded behind her as she ran down the stairs. Her Coptic grandmother (the mother of her mother), used to warn her against leaping down the stairs, or riding bicycles, or stamping with her feet on the ground, or taking big strides when she walked.

– The honour[1] of a girl is as fine and delicate as cigarette paper.

Every time a cigarette burned out between the lips of her father or her grandfather, or the stub was thrown away, she imagined that she was the burning end that had been thrown away amidst the ashes.

– Ganat, wake up.

A hand nudged her on the shoulder. But she was fast asleep and one hand was not enough to wake her up. Her sleep was deep, total, encompassing, almost akin to death. She was very aware of death. She could feel it within her. She watched herself as she died. She could see her father sitting with the Koran in his hands.

[1] The hymen.

His voice was choking as though there were something in his throat, and he was trying to clear it.

– Nothing can wash away dishonour except death.

The air was heavy with smoke, with the weight of defeat. Around her neck was a belt. It was tight. It was choking her. Was it she who was choking herself? Whatever had happened to her, it could not kill her. How could she die if the brain in her head were still working? It was someone else's hand that was trying to drag her to death, to lead her towards it. Perhaps it was the hand of God. It could be her father, or her husband, or her grandfather, dead before she was born. But his soul had risen from the grave in order to wash away the stain of dishonour.

She half-opened her eyelids as though hiding from herself as she took a furtive look at what was happening around her. She saw the grandfather she had never seen before. His soul was clad in the *caftan*[I] of Sheikh Bassiouni. His turban had been wound round his head several times. He was standing in the dark behind a clothes-stand. His voice was strange, yet familiar with a hoarse note in it. He was talking in the classical language:

– Stand with your face to the wall and lift your hands above your head.

This was the way in which they were punished at

[I] A long, collarless open coat more like a robe worn over the usual clothing of religious dignitaries and rural gentry.

school. So she stood with her face close to the wall, and her arms raised up. She felt her clothes being lifted from behind, and something like a finger creeping between her buttocks, but she dared not drop an arm. Her body was seized with contractions and her arm dropped down by itself. Immediately the cane landed on her. She lifted her arm quickly, using her other hand to hold it up as far as it would go towards the ceiling.

The bell rang and the class emptied itself. No one was left except her. She continued to stand up against the wall making an effort so that her arms would not drop. In her dreams she remained upright, her body never bending or bowing or drooping no matter how savagely the stick landed on her. She was doing exactly what her grandmother (the mother of her father) had taught her to do.

– Why are you standing like that Sitti El Haja?[1]

– So that when Azrail[2] arrives he will find me standing.

She did not know who Azrail was. Her grandmother said he came at night while one was asleep to steal one's soul away from the body. So if he came and found her wide awake standing on her feet he would go to another woman.

– Another woman?

[1] A term of respect for an old woman. Literally, my mistress who has done the pilgrimage to Mecca.
[2] The angel of death.

The words echoed in her ears like two gunshots, one shot after the other. Then there was a silence, a complete silence. Nothing could be heard except the distant barking of a dog. The horn of a car sounded just once. On the wall nothing remained except a circular patch of light creeping across it. It climbed up the wall to the ceiling, dropped down to the ground, moved slowly over the tiled floor, rose up on to the bed, crossed over to her face, and stopped over her lids.

She half-opened her eyes. The Director was leaning over her. The Head Nurse stood close to him. He wrote something down on a piece of paper. The Head Nurse nodded her bent head and said:

– We will execute your orders.

The Director turned round and walked out of the room. She followed him with bent shoulders. Before closing the door behind her she turned round.

– Narguiss?

The Head Nurse's lips opened and emitted a series of sounds like the mewing of a cat, or the sobs of someone weeping. Then the sounds died away in the air.

The door closed and the room was plunged into darkness. She heard the key turn round in the lock three times, and steps running down the tiled corridor. A sound of heels clicking and of breath panting.

4 *Narguiss*

She reached her room on the upper floor, went in quickly, and closed the door behind her. Her breath was still coming in gasps. She leaned her back against the wall and closed her eyes. Two small girls were playing hopscotch in the yard of the school. They ran out into the green fields chasing after the butterflies. She opened her eyes and found herself standing in front of the mirror. She removed the veil from around her head and her black hair dropped down to her shoulders in two long plaits like a schoolgirl. She shook her head. The plaits shook with it.

– Narguiss.

Her voice sounded strangely in her ears. The name Narguiss sounded even stranger, like the name of some other woman who was standing upright against the wall close to her.

– Was she Narguiss or some spirit which had taken over her body?

She believed in spirits. Genii had been mentioned

in the Koran. That's what her father had said to her. Her grandmother kept telling her about the spirit of her grandfather that came out of his grave at night. It walked over the earth without arms or legs, without anything which the eye could see. Sometimes it took on the body of a cat and squatted in front of the door of the water-closet or the House of Good Manners as her grandmother called it. There it would shed the body of the cat and creep into that of a mouse, or a lizard, or remain what it was, just a spirit without body, capable of slipping under the edge of the door or the window.

She was afraid of these spirits and genii. She woke up in the middle of the night to make sure that the window was well shut. Then she stuffed up the slit between the window and the ledge with a rag, or a page torn out of her copy book. Once back in bed she enveloped herself from head to foot in the eiderdown, leaving not the slightest opening through which the spirit could steal in. She slept with her knees held together, her thighs closed so tightly that no human being or spirit could ever separate between them.

She stood in front of the mirror and gazed into her dark face. Her thin body was clad in a long white dress. The other woman on the wall was wearing black and her shoulders drooped like her grandmother's. She turned away from the mirror and stepped back. The shadow on the wall took a step backwards with her. Was she the woman in the mirror or the one on the wall? On her breast lay the Medal of Honour and Love for her Country of the first order. It was a golden disc attached by a pin. She undid it from her dress and laid it in a box lined with green velvet. She patted the box, then put it in a drawer. She slipped out of her dress, letting it drop to the floor in a little heap. She glimpsed her breasts in the mirror and quickly hid them with her hands. She covered her shoulders with a large white shawl, and took a sip of water from the glass near her bed. Her mouth felt dry and her heart was pounding. Something buried within her filled her with fear, something unknown imprisoned inside. A voice unlike any human voice hissed in her ear.

Was it the Devil whispering in her ear?

She went over to the window and looked up at the sky. It was a deep black. There was no moon, nor were there any stars except for a single bright star visible in the distance. Her grandmother used to sing a song to the star. The song said:

– O, Zahra,[1] mother of the Universe, and the trees would move like evil spirits in the night.

She glimpsed him sitting behind the tall stump of a tree-trunk, his body enveloped in the wide folds of his white *gallabeya*. His head was swathed in a turban in the form of a cone, like a dunce's cap, and it was

[1] Literally in Arabic, flower. The planet is Venus.

topped with a peacock's feather. His face was raised to the sky, and he was gazing into space, while all the time his lips were opening and closing as though he were repeating a verse of the Koran, or murmuring something to himself.

He saw her standing at the window and immediately curled up around himself like a porcupine. He was more afraid of her than he was of the Director. She was a woman, and inside him was a deep-seated fear of women. His head had been caught between the pelvic bones of his mother as she was giving birth to him. She had pressed her thigh bones tightly together and almost crushed him to death before he had time to be born. He knew she had not wanted him to live. She could not stand the sight of his nose. It reminded her of his father. The Head Nurse was a boss and deep down inside him he also had a fear of bosses. One day his father returned home deathly pale. He went to bed delirious with fever. At night he could hear him gasp out one word:

– The Boss.[1]

Before the early morning call to prayer rang out he was dead.

He curled his body round himself behind the trunk of the tree. His head was hidden between his knees. She stood at the window and all she could see of him was a dark shadow squatting on the ground. Her lips

[1] Here the ruler, the President.

were parted in a smile and her mouth was twisted a little towards the right. The mouth of the Director had the same twist when he smiled, and the boss of the Director too. All the bosses or rulers whose pictures she saw in the newspapers had this smile, and all of them had mouths which twisted to the right side when they smiled. The twist had a certain aura about it, something which had to do with the high status of the person concerned.

She took a deep breath, filling her chest with air. Her father's chest swelled like that when he sat next to the Headman of the Village and crossed his legs. No one ever sat next to the Headman and crossed his legs like that,[1] only her father after he became the barber of the King. Men started to bow their heads to him as though they were seeing the King himself. They could not believe it possible that a man from their village could encounter the King face to face without any one in between, and could hold his chin between his hands and pass a razor over it. After the country ceased to be a kingdom he no longer crossed his legs in the presence of the Headman but he would lift his head high whenever he spoke of his daughter. How she stood in front of the President on Victory Day. How she bowed down with the upper half of her body and moved out her hand to shake that of the President.

[1] To keep one's legs down in the traditional culture is a sign of respect, even awe.

How she hung the Medal of Honour and Love of Country around her neck.

– Honour.

Her father's voice rang out as he pronounced the word. He opened his mouth as wide as he could to let it out, as though he were yawning. He rolled it with his tongue pronouncing the two syllables separately. They seemed to fly out from his mouth together with drops of saliva. The ears of the women sitting in the shelter of the river bank picked them up as they echoed sharply. Their bodies shrunk into their *gallabeyas* at the sound. They held their knees and thighs closely together, leaving no space. They muttered words from the Koran to chase away devils and evil spirits. Honour meant chastity, and chastity was more valued than land. The men inherited it in a line from father to son. No one would dare as much as to touch someone else's honour, be he a spirit, or a genie with powers above those of ordinary men. The stigma of dishonour, of losing one's honour, could only be washed off by blood. And blood alone was the mark of an intact honour[1] on the wedding night. The *daya*[2] would be there with her finger tapering into a long sharp tip at the nail which she plunged into the fine membrane. Blood poured out on to the white towel which was

[1] An intact hymen preserves the honour of the family and especially of the men in the family.
[2] Rural midwife.

held high to flutter above people's heads. The women let out a chorus of shrill *you yous* and the drums beat. The breasts of the men and the husbands could now swell and their noses rise as high as the ceiling above. For honour meant the honour of the male, even if the proof of it was in the body of the female.

That night when the towel rose over their heads, as white as milk without the smallest drop of blood on it, that night everything was pitch dark. The body of the King's barber shrank into itself and into his seat. His neck had become so short, so thin, that it was no bigger than a sesame seed.[1] He rose from his bed in the middle of the night, opened the wooden box where he kept his barber's kit and took out the razor. He sharpened it on a whetstone. In the morning they found him lying in a pool of blood with the white towel soaked in it. He had saved his honour. It was now intact.

She moved from the mirror to the window and stood looking at her face in it. Her eyelids were swollen and around them ran a web of wrinkles. Her cheeks were sunken, their flesh flabby. There had been a time when they were full and smooth, and when she had a gleam in her eye. She had changed from a child into an ageing woman overnight, on the night which people called the Night of Happiness.[2] She could not remember

[1] Popularly used to indicate an inability to hold one's head high.
[2] In Arabic, Farah, which means a wedding night.

anything in her life called youth, or go back to a time when she day-dreamed. She had never known what it meant to have an adolescence. Her sisters and her school mates and all the village girls were like that. Her head dropped out of her mother's belly on to a piece of land which was called their country, and there was nothing else.

She shivered as though with fever. The word *country* expressed for her a deep love. She had learnt to write the four letters *Misr*[1] even before she could write her name. When she asked her teacher what the word *country* meant he said it was the land on which she trod. Her heart sagged with the weight of the love she had for it. It was owned by the Headman of the Village but her mother toiled on it. She went out in demonstrations with her school mates and they shouted:

– Long live our Country; long live our Land.

Her heart burned passionately with the love she had for the word *country*, which was composed of seven letters, neither more nor less. She repeated it to herself over and over again until it was inscribed in her memory. When she spoke of it her heart ventured far from her lips, and her mind strayed even further from her heart when she shouted the word out loud on the streets. Her body moved with a will of its own as she walked down the streets, or stood on the pavement.

[1] Egypt in Arabic.

She found herself turning back to the place where she had started out, walking with a heavy step towards her father who was buried there, who was dead. Her mind kept telling her that he was no longer alive, that he was dead, but she still kept going back to hold his hand and kiss it. She swore to him three times in the name of God the Great that she was innocent. No one had ever touched her. Neither a human being nor a devil, not even a spirit. No one at all, either in her dreams or in her waking hours. She swore that ever since she was a child she had always closed the window tight, stuffed the cracks in the walls and the door with rags, plugged her ears so that she could not hear the whispering of the Devil, or even the sighing of the wind. She had kept her knees tightly pressed together so that no human hand or even spirit could push one leg away from the other. But her father's voice kept coming back in broken tones.

– But daughter, why then was there no blood?

She turned her eyes upwards to the heavens and asked:

– Tell me, God, where was the blood?

There was complete silence. Nobody answered. She could hear the distant horn of a car. The air was still. The heads of the trees stood motionless. One leaf dropped from a branch to the ground. Then nothing. Not a single sound in the night.

– Where was the blood, o God?

She repeated the question. She never tired of repeating it. She had great hopes of God. He was just,
and He was merciful, and He would never let her
down. She strained her ears to hear His voice. She
heard whispering. It was like the sighing of the wind
in the night.

– A plot. The Headman's plot.

– But why, o God?

– He wanted to revenge himself on your father.

– Why?

– Your father used to sit opposite him and cross
one leg over the other.

– O God, and why not?

– People belong to different levels. The eye cannot
rise above the brow.[1]

– People are born equal. They are like the teeth of
a comb.[2]

– You dare to answer me, you brazen girl?

– I . . . brazen . . . God.

– Shut your mouth, and not one more word.

– I . . .

– Don't interrupt me.

– . . .

– Don't dare to raise your eyes to me.

– . . .

– You've inherited your father's conceit.

[1] This is an Egyptian proverb.
[2] The Prophet Mohammed's words.

She groped for her father's hand in the dark. She knew he was dead but she could still feel his hand. She kissed it. The smell she knew so well penetrated her nose. It flowed in her veins like blood. She used to think it was the odour of God. She could detect it when she sat next to her father, the smell that would come from his sitting with the Koran between his hands. He nodded his head and read some of its verses aloud. She had not yet learned how to read, just turned the pages with her fingers and looked at the letters. She sniffed the odour of the pages; they were so fine that they almost tore between her fingers. Her father hit her hand.

– It's God's book, you little ass.

It was the only book her father had in the house. He kept it on the shelf above the wooden box containing his barber's kit. Before he touched it he did his ablutions, and washed his hands five times. He knew it all by heart from beginning to end and was always reciting it whether by day or night. He kneeled before God with the book in his hands.

– O God, my father never missed a single prayer.

– I know that Narguiss.

– Why then did you do that to me?

– I wanted to test your faith, you stupid ass.

– My father was a firm believer. He never doubted.

She bowed her head to the ground. In her imagination she could see the Prophet Abraham preparing to sacrifice his son. The sacrificial lamb had not yet been sent down. She raised her tear-filled eyes to the heavens. Her father was better than the Prophet Abraham. He had sacrificed himself for his daughter.

Her mother too had been a devout woman, a virgin throughout her life just like the Virgin Mary. But her grandmother was the best amongst all of them. She laboured all day in the fields, and at night she spent hours in prayer.

In the mirror she could see the tears running down her face. She dried them with a corner of the shawl, and it slipped off one shoulder revealing her breast. She put out her hand quickly and lifted it back. The eyes of the Director peered at her from the wall, and she hid from them behind the door of the cupboard. His eyes were everywhere like those of all Directors. She threw a pillow at him and her shawl fell to the ground. She glimpsed her naked body in the mirror, ran to the lamp, switched it off, and jumped into bed, pulling the covers over her head. His fingers were big, covered in pallid hairs, and his voice was like the voice of all Directors with a note of sarcasm piercing through.

– Are you shy, girl?

She made a noise like the moaning of a cat. Miaou, miaou, miaou.

– Is it the shyness of virgins, girl, or what?

She shrank under the covers not daring to look at

him. Since she had come to the palace she had not dared to raise her eyes to his. He was the big Director. As soon as she walked in his eyes went to her breasts. And when she turned round to go out through the door she felt his eyes lingering on her buttocks. She fought to get rid of his eyes the way she did with the Devil's voice when it whispered to her. On a winter's night he came into her room. She put her head on his chest and burst into tears.

— I swear I am a virgin, sir.

— How come, girl?

— There was no blood, sir.

— Maybe your hymen is elastic, girl.

— What does elastic mean?

— It means like an elastic band.

He laughed, and his laugh was so loud that it made the legs of the bed shake. His laugh echoed in her ears and her legs trembled under her. Elastic. It was a word that ended in a sharp tip and it pierced her ear. The Director gave her a lesson in anatomy. He pulled the pen out of his top pocket, and drew the opening of the vagina, and the hymen, on a piece of paper.

— It is God in His wisdom who created the elastic hymen. Elastic means capable of stretching, not too rigid. And elasticity is a quality which is often required, said the Director.

When she looked into the mirror she could see that a tear had dried in her eye. A faint light shone from the lamp near her bed. She stretched out her hand and switched it off. Her body vanished in the dark together with that of the Director, and everything disappeared into nothing.

5 *A Fight in the Night*

He was curled up like a porcupine behind the trunk of the tree. He watched her shadow come and go behind the window. Her breasts kept appearing and disappearing under the shawl. Her breathing was deep, prolonged like an exhortation or a sigh.

– O God.

He was on the verge of coming out into the open, and revealing himself, but he knew that she was the Head Nurse, not Nefissa or any of the other women in the female ward. Between him and women who were in charge of something or other there was a long-standing feud. It had been like that ever since his mother had squeezed his head between her pelvic bones. After that, when he was still small, and she was big, the palm of her hand used to land on his cheek like an axe. He hid from her in the cupboard, suffocating with the smell of her clothes, as they hung down over his head, with the odours of dried sweat and milk, with the rattle of bracelets and bangles, with raw chewing gum, and red henna, and sanitary napkins. From behind the cupboard door he could hear her voice call out:

– Zakaria.

The name sounded strange to his ears as though he had never heard it before, and yet somehow familiar as though he had been hearing it all his life. Zakaria? He wondered if the name meant anything. He dismissed the sound from his mind and with it the image of his mother, and his wife, and all women. Deep down inside him he felt a deep revulsion for the other sex, but with it was mingled another feeling, one of attraction. His eyes were drawn to every woman who did not resemble his mother. He chose women who were small in size, whose bones were frail and whose hands were too flabby and soft to slap. But the image of his mother never abandoned him. The smell of her body dwelt in his nose. It evoked a deep yearning for her. He longed to throw himself into her arms, into the arms of every woman who resembled her.

– O God.

His ears appeared on either side of the tree-trunk. He strained his hearing. A devout, humble, female voice called out to him. It was not at all like the haughty, imperious voice of the Head Nurse. His eyes fastened themselves on her window. He was attracted to her despite his revulsion. She was the only one amongst all these women who refused to recognise him, to believe in him. She watched him in the same way as his mother had done, looked at him with eyes like those of his wife. She had beaten him on the tips of his fingers, made him stand with his face to the wall, or turned her back to him in bed.

– O . . . God.

The voice ceased and the light was switched off in her room. He waited a little while to make sure that she had fallen asleep, then emerged from his hiding place. He was tall and stood upright, holding his head proudly, wearing a big turban with a feather at the top which rose up in the dark like a bayonet from a gun. He walked with a slow step. The trees seemed to bend their heads to him, the earth and the sky to stretch themselves out humbly at his feet.

He nodded his head, satisfied with the universe, with things as they were. He had created it in six days and rested on the seventh day of the week. That's what the men in the ward had said but then they skipped the last part and added in its place:

– You do not toil the way we do. You do not know what weariness is, so you should not know any rest.

His big feet were shod in a pair of rubber slippers. He waved his hand over his face as though chasing away flies and placed one foot after the other on the ground with a slow, weighty tread. Under his feet lay a long red carpet which stretched right up to the horizon. The round disc of the sun burned in the sky above the Pyramid of Khoufou. He could see his image reflected in the disc, recognised his face despite the huge distance. His face was big, and square like that of a hyena. His eyebrows were bushy and met over the bridge of his nose. It was a big cartilaginous hook like the beak of an eagle. Right from the beginning, from the first moment he saw it in the mirror, he had wanted to be rid of it, but it was rooted firm and deep in his head. His ears, too, were not like those of human beings. They were curled forwards like the horns in the head of a cow or a calf.

He pouted his lips in scorn, smiled in a secretive way which only reached one corner of his mouth. The calf was a sacred calf and he used to make drawings of it in his school copy book. It carried the sun on its horns and had two breasts like his mother. They called out to it using a woman's name, Hathour[1] or Satour,[2] just as his grandmother did.

– You there . . . You . . . You . . .

He stopped for a moment and listened to the voice calling out. The whistling in his ears grew louder, growing like the roar of a waterfall to which he came nearer, like thousands of voices shouting.

– Long live . . . Long live . . .

The voices fused into a single voice. All the people were shouting, and all the people were as silent as

[1] and [2] The names of angels.

death. He walked down between two lines of soldiers which stretched out on either side as far as the eye could see. They gave him the military salute, and he responded with his right arm lifted up. His right leg also went up in the air like a wooden stick, with, at its foot, a long black leather tip which shone in the light and a high iron heel shaped like the shoe of a horse. He held it up in the air for a long moment, then let it drop close to the other leg. The drums of victory beat out the military march. Thousands of soldiers hit the ground with their feet in a unified step. They lifted their legs in the air, holding them stiff like sticks, and bringing them down together. Their faces were grey like the stones of the Mokattam Hills, their noses stood out, one nose behind the other, in a straight line to infinity. Their heads, closely shaven under their brass helmets, touched each other as they advanced. Under each helmet was a pair of eyes sunken so deep in their orbits that they seemed to turn over themselves to look inside. Their mouths were open as though gasping for breath, and the pupils of their eyes were hidden under half-closed lids.

– Long life to him. May he live forever.

He sucked in the word *forever* through every opening in his head, through his eyes, and his nose, and his mouth, and through his ears which stood up and opened their flaps, and through the pores of his body, through whatever openings he had. He sucked in the word, absorbed it right into his flesh. Its letters were like drops of water to a thirsty man. He licked them up with his tongue, chewed on them in his mouth, and shook his head with satisfaction. A smile hovered over his lips, his mouth twisted itself to the right, then went back to its usual place.

Then the voices ceased their shouting and were replaced by a woman singing:

– My beloved country. My love for you is great. My love for you is a burning fire.

Her body could be seen up on the high platform, her flesh shivering and shaking under the dancer's dress. She jerked like a silver fish in a net, like a mermaid risen from the depths. She twisted and moaned with eyes closed in an ecstatic trance. Her name was now Zouzou but when she started out she was known as Zanouba.

And the chorus answered back:

– A burning fire, my love! A burning fire!

He followed her out of the corner of his eye without moving his head. She winked at him, sending a coded message which no one could catch. He was very cautious. He had a wife whose eyes were open wide and stared without a blink. He washed himself five times with soap and water before he came home at night. She looked at him in the dark as he tiptoed in. He faced the wall and turned his back to her. But her nose reached out and smelt the odour in his underpants before he had time to undress. Her eyes were two black discs of fire that stung his neck as he slept. Her voice was like a burning wind when she said:

– You've fallen. Low.

The word *fallen* pierced his ear like a shot. It was a word that was never heard on a woman's lips unless she was speaking to a child of hers who had done something wrong. Her voice reminded him of his mother. The tip of her tongue darted out between her lips at the end of the word like a sting. Her mouth opened wide as she let the word out, then it shut tight over clenched teeth.

– Fallen. Low.

The word lodged itself at the back of his head like a bullet. It slipped down like a small steel ball-bearing which revolved around itself. Fallen! Low! In the school grammar book he read the word *fell*. It was a verb in the past tense and *fallen* was the past participle which was used in the plural for women. Fallen women. In the language there was no masculine plural. It was not used. Nor did it exist in the history books, or the holy books. Adam was not described as a fallen man. A man only *fell* in a test, or in the elections, or in a battle, or as a boy in school examinations.

– Fallen. Low.

He lifted his hand high up in the air preparing to land it on her face, but she was quicker than him. Her body moved faster, rose in the air like a butterfly. She was young, and he was old, moved slowly. His hair had fallen out and his eyelashes, too. His pupils were misty and he could not see the world around him clearly. His eyes went round looking for her but she had disappeared in the dark like a drop of water in the sea. A second ago she had been right here but now she was gone. She had been here for thirty years, walking by his side down the lines of soldiers standing to attention. The music played an anthem to victory. He left her standing at the back with the other women, and walked on to the front where the platform stood. He bowed as they gave him the medal for heroes. They pinned it on his chest. It was a golden disc that shone in the light. He walked with a slow step, his head held up. Up! Up! Up! A voice echoed from afar. It seemed to travel right across the world, rise up to the heavens. Up! Up! Up! Up to the top. I am at the top, right at the top.

His eyes glanced around him as he walked, and the voice kept echoing in his ears like the wind. I am on top! Right at the top! His eyes were fixed on the heavens. The turban was wound around his head with the feather at the top, and his shadow lay on the ground, dark and long. His neck rose straight up. His nose was as pointed and sharp as a needle. He walked slowly to the back door of the palace, climbed up the stairs step by step, and halted on the landing. A faint light gleamed in his eyes.

His eyes were small and round, and the cornea of each eye was slightly raised, as though it were carved out of something solid, like a round stone. His gaze was steady, and rested quietly on their outer surface, but something seemed to move underneath like a drop of moisture, or a tear imprisoned, trying to break loose. Each lid was a dark swelling and the face was square like Aboul Houl.[1]

He moved his jaws as though chewing and swallowed dryly, with an effort, his Adam's apple jerking up and down his throat. It stood out prominently like something he could not swallow. It was a rotten evil apple and should have stopped in Eve's throat not in that of Adam's. That was what his grandfather had once said to him.

He stopped at the door of the male ward, straightened the turban with its feather, and filled his chest with air.

– I am right at the top, above everybody else, he said to himself.

He pushed open the door and walked in. The ward was plunged in silence, enveloped in darkness with the beds arranged in straight rows, and the bodies lying on them deep in sleep. He surveyed them from a height, held his nose up in the air. They were his creatures and that was what he called them – his

[1] The Sphinx

creatures. At night they slept. He alone did not sleep
at night.

He walked down between the rows of beds, turning
his head first to one side and then to the other. His
mouth twisted in a smile. Everything was in order. No
one dared disobey him, or stray from the universal fold.
They were all fast asleep with their eyes tightly closed.

He came to a sudden stop. He had noticed two eyes
wide open and staring at him. The eyelashes stood out
thickly and the pupils were a gleaming black. The hair
on his head was unshaven, long and thick, and also
black. A rebellious lock fell over his forehead. He
recognised him at once. It was Eblis. It could not be
anyone else. He walked up to him slowly, stopped to
gaze at him for a long moment, then nudged him in
the shoulder with his long pointed finger.

– You awake, boy?

He did not answer. He lay on the bed without moving, his eyes fixed on the ceiling, as though no one had
spoken to him. He seemed to be deep in thought. In
front of his eyes was an image that refused to disappear. The big iron gate swung open, and she burst in,
a gust of wind throwing her hair backwards, like a
rebellious mare refusing to be tamed. Her large eyes
were open and looked straight ahead. Their look was
penetrating like the sharp point of a rapier. But below
their surface was the soft gleam he caught in his
mother's eyes sometimes.

– Answer me, boy.

His lips remained tightly closed. No sound emerged from them. Since the moment he had seen her come in, the memory of his mother kept returning to him. Her body was tall, straight as an arrow. When she crossed in front of the Headman of the Village she never bowed her head. The heads of the men were bent, and their eyes looked at the ground, but she always walked with her head erect, her eyes looking straight ahead. Her foot was big, and bare like the Prophet's foot, and she trod on it with all her weight. Her bones were big and when she hit the ground with her hoe the earth split open. Her voice echoed in his ears with a moaning sound like the wind:

– Never bend your head in front of that man like your father did.

After that his father lay in the house and never went out until the day he died of fever in his bed.

The women slapped their cheeks, and shrieked and wept. She washed her hair and tied it with a white scarf, then took him by the hand to the village school. On the way she bought him a pencil and a copy book.

– Speak up, you devil!

Eblis saw him standing in the dark, his big head swathed in the turban, his eyes under it small and shining like those of Sheikh Masoud. Sheikh Masoud beat him on the tips of his fingers, and asked him to

recite the Sourat[1] of the Angels. He did not know how
to write, but he knew the verses by heart. He repeated
them in a low voice with his eyes closed:

– *And God said unto the angels and I shall appoint a
viceroy[2] to rule on the earth. And the angels asked Him
dost thou appoint he who will cause bloodshed and sow
evil? Do we not sing thy praises, o Lord?*

– What is the name of the ruler, boy?

He stared at the ceiling unable to find the answer.
His mother's voice whispered in his ear.

– He's called the Headman, my son.

He closed his eyes. He could see the angels standing
behind one another dressed in their white garments.
They repeated in one voice:

– *Dost thou appoint he who will sow evil?*

The voice resounded in his ears like the roar of a
waterfall.

– Down with the evil viceroy.

He opened his eyes and whispered to the boy seated
next to him.

– He's called the Headman, not the viceroy.

– Headman? What Headman? That was years ago.

– At the time of the King?

– What King?

– You seem to be living in another world.

– Then what's he called now?

[1] Chapter in the Koran.
[2] Caliph or Khalifa in Arabic.

– Now they call him the General.

He pressed his lips tightly together, closed his eyes and hid his head under the bedcovers. He felt a finger prod his shoulder.

– Don't you know who I am, boy?

He looked out from under the bedcovers and stared at the face in front of him with wide-open eyes. The features were familiar. The nose was like that of Sheikh Masoud. The face was square-shaped, white-skinned with a red flush over the cheeks like the face of the General. But the language he spoke was Arabic.

– Don't you know who I am, Eblis?

He opened his lips and said in a faint voice:

– I know Your Grace.

He prodded him again in the shoulder.

– Say *Your Grace* to the Headman or to the Director but not to me. I am above everyone else. Is that clear?

– It's clear, sir.

– Sir, your ass. Say, yes my Lord God.

– Yes my Lord God. But give me a chance to get some sleep.

– Sleep?! What do you mean sleep, you devil. Who will go around whispering into people's ears and leading them into temptation if you're going to sleep, Eblis?

He shut his eyes and turned over on his side with his back toward him. But the long pointed finger prodded him again.

– Get up at once, boy, and get busy.

– Let me sleep. I'm dead tired.

– Get up I tell you. Go and whisper in people's ears, boy.

– And if I don't whisper what will happen? Why not let everybody go to heaven?

– Then for whom will I have created Hell, you ass?

– You can roast sheep in it. What's wrong with that, my friend?

– What's that you're calling me, boy? Have you forgotten who I am?

– I apologise, Lord God. Don't be angry! You're not my friend or anything of the sort. You're my Lord. You're my King. I bow down to you. Come let me kiss you on your head and ask for forgiveness.

Eblis leapt out of his bed and rushed towards him ready to kiss him on the head. The turban he was wearing rolled to the ground together with the feather. His closely shaven head was bared. Eblis touched it with his lips, his laughter ringing out in joyful peals.

The men lying on their beds in the ward woke up. They looked around, opening their eyes wide as though they had suddenly awakened from death, and were entering another world. Eblis and God were now fighting hand to hand, raining blows on one another. Curses resounded in the air. The curses stopped and they went for one another again with punches and slaps. The men sat around on their beds, dressed in their white garments, looking on with listless eyes, but below the surface was a silent gleam like children or young people who were watching some competition. They started to clap and shout words of encouragement:

– Heh! heh! heh! heh!

All except one man. His body was small and shrunken, and his face was covered in wrinkles. He had a toothless mouth and his big eyes bulged behind his spectacles. His head was completely bald, and he had a long white beard which straggled down limply over his chest. Under his arm he carried a book. He advanced slowly on his bare feet towards the two men who were fighting. He lifted a meagre arm like an old cotton stick and called out in a piping voice:

– The court is in session.

There was a sudden silence. Eblis stood stock-still and God followed suit, dropping his arms to his side. All eyes were now staring at the old man. This time his voice was so loud that when it rang out the walls seemed to shake.

– The court is in session.

The men looked at one another. They nodded their heads in silence. Some of them got up and started to push the beds aside. They set up a small platform in the middle and covered it with a white sheet. On the sheet they placed a glass of water and a hammer for the man with the wrinkled face, then they dropped a black cloak on his shoulders. He was now the judge. His voice resounded again.

– The court is in session.

Suddenly a whistle echoed in the corridor with a long shrilling noise. Behind the glass panels they glimpsed the shadow of the Head Nurse, and beside her one of the male nurses walking in step. The platform disappeared and with it the judge with the wrinkled face. The ward was plunged again into darkness and a total silence reigned. Not a movement, not a sound could be heard in the ward, only a black feather lying on the floor which shifted gently in a draught of air.

6 *Nefissa*

She heard the whistle blow as she lay in the female ward. It echoed in her ears like the whistling of the wind. She opened her eyes, and looked around. She could see rows of heads enveloped in white veils. They rested on the pillows, fast asleep. Their breathing gave out snoring or moaning sounds. When they moaned it reminded her of her mother moaning at night. A long, drawn-out call like the howl of a distant wind:

– Yahou – yahou – yahou.

A long, thin snake slithered over the wall. Its body was yellow, its head black. The eyes were small and the mouth protruded, tapering at the tip. The snake blew out air and the air made a whistling sound which resembled her name:

– Nefissa.

Her eyes opened wide in surprise. Could a snake make sounds which were human? Could it call out her name? How could it pick her out from among the other women, know that she was Nefissa?

She stared at the snake for a long moment, then covered her face with her hands.

– *I seek refuge in Thee o God from the evil of the Devil.*

She muttered the verse of the Seat to chase away the spirits, undid the belt tied around her chest, and stood up. The windows of the ward were closed, and the air was still. She felt her soul suffocating in her body, struggling to find a way out. She opened the window, glimpsed the sky and the earth like one single expanse with no stars and no moon. Only one star cut through space with its steady light. The voice of her mother reached her from afar.

– Where is my son, o Zahra, mother of justice and mercy?

Her mother stood in the dark. Her back was towards her, and her face was to the window. The sound of her breathing could be heard as her chest rose and fell.

– Where is my son, o Zahra, where?

Her voice wafted through the silence of the night. It reached the ears of Sheikh Masoud as he advanced in the narrow lane. He stopped suddenly as though some spirit had pounced on him, tapped the earth with his stick, and spat on the ground:

– God's curse be upon you, whore that you are!

She thought he was cursing her mother. He said it was another woman he was cursing, another woman called Zahra who had fallen from heaven and thrown a spell over the spirits of Harout and Marout to use them to her ends. She asked her mother who Harout and Marout were and her mother said they were spirits which came out at night. Then the she-goat gave birth to twins and her mother named them Harout and Marout. But Harout died, and Marout kept staring at her with his red eyes as though she were the cause of his brother's death. So whenever her mother left the house to go somewhere, she would hold on to her skirt as tight as she could. Her mother had big feet, and she took long strides when she walked. She kept falling flat on her face trying to keep up with her. Her nose and mouth became choked with dust, and she might easily have lost her on the way, but she held tightly to the skirt and never let go even for an instant. At night she slept in her mother's embrace with her arms around her and her eyelids tightly closed. She was scared to open her eyes, in case when she opened them she might not find her mother lying by her side.

– Where is my son, Zahra, mother of justice and mercy?

The night was like a dark cloud which had enveloped the whole world. There was neither moon in the sky nor stars. Just one star up there like an eye which remained on vigil, keeping guard. It looked down on her from far away as she lay in her mother's embrace. She slept on her right side with her arm under her head. The air smelt of earth sprayed with water. The she-ass lay in the entrance door to the house with her four legs stretched out. The goat slept with its eyes closed, but the cat squatted with its head up and its eyes wide open. In the dark they were bright green, the colour of the fields.

– Where has my son gone, Zahra?

Her mother never stopped repeating this question all through the night. When she fell asleep the same words could be heard coming out from her mouth with her breathing. When she walked her feet beat out the same rhythm on the ground. Her lips were always tightly closed and her eyes scanned the heavens. Her head was always held up despite the sack of cotton she carried on her neck and shoulders. She followed behind her, trotting on her tiny legs, holding on tightly to her mother's skirt. The sun was glaringly hot and the ground burnt the soles of her feet. Thick clouds of dust swirled up between the ambling legs of the cows and buffaloes. From under their tails dropped urine and sweat, and small, round, dark blobs of dung that dried under the sun, and lay along the road wherever they went. She closed her eyes imagining the mat laid out over the floor which had been sprinkled with water. To her it was like a dream, like the Paradise of Eden which her mother had told her about when she could barely walk. Her lips would open to gasp out the words Paradise of Eden as she lay panting in the entrance to their house after they came back.

– Paradise of Eden.

Two words that she never stopped repeating in her sleep. She did not ask her mother where the Paradise of Eden was. She never asked questions. She was supposed to believe everything she heard without question. That was what Sheikh Masoud kept saying.

– Everything, you slip of a girl, Nefissa, or else you'll land in hellfire with the Devil.

She did not know who the Devil was. She thought he was her younger brother. Her mother gave birth to him two years after she was born. She bought him a copy book and a pencil. From the day when he went to the village school Sheikh Masoud never stopped calling him by the name Eblis. He beat him on the soles of his feet with his cane and the boy would hide from him in the mud-oven.

At night he lay next to her on the mat. She could hear him sobbing quietly. She wound her arms around him until morning, and in winter they would sleep together under the same scanty cover. The cold wind came in through the cracks of the window. She closed her eyes and dreamed of a thick cotton eiderdown. The dreams of girls in the village never went beyond a thick cotton eiderdown. She had learnt the word *cotton* early on. Her mother planted cotton and carried sacks of it on her head. The sacks were stored in the Headman's house and next day they disappeared. No one knew where they went.

Then one day the Head of the village guard turned

up and knocked at the door of their house with the butt of his rifle. Her brother hid himself in his mother's arms but the Head Guard pulled him away from her and poked him in the shoulder with the bayonet:

– Come on you, Eblis, off to national service.

– National service!

The Head Guard stood in the courtyard of their house wearing a uniform the colour of dust. Hanging from it were brass buttons, coated with rust. His face was as grey as ash, and his skin was covered with pimples and small craters. He closed his lids and opened his mouth as he pronounced the words *national service*. He had big solid jaws like a huge pair of scissors or pincers. He intoned the *n* and the *a* with a long drawn-out sound, closing his eyes and opening his mouth, then opened his eyes to end the word with a sharp *l* which made the tip of his tongue emerge from between his lips. He ended the phrase by clenching his jaws as though there was nothing more to be said. The words *national service* made the women wind their arms around their sons and hide them in their folded bodies as though they were trying to draw them back into their bellies.

Since the time of the Pharaohs the words *national service* had always meant death. A woman would give birth to a male child and then give him up as a sacrifice to the god. The god sat on his golden throne surrounded by his soldiers. People saw his picture later in the newspapers, and he was called by a different name at different times. The names and words changed but the throne was the same. The lines of soldiers were always there too. The uniforms, the material from which they were made, the buttons tightly fastened over the chest, the shoulder straps and the insignia changed, but nothing else. Boys were still called up by orders which came from above, written on a piece of paper with the stamp of the eagle on it. It smelt of gunpowder, of old tanned leather in a printing press, of dust from the carpets lying on the floor of a musty office with pictures in golden frames hanging on the walls. His head hung on the wall. It never moved. Its eyes looked out of the square, hyena-like face into space. Its lips were slightly parted in a smile which twisted the mouth to one side.

– National service, boy!

His mother undid the white scarf that was tied around her head. She undid the tresses of her long black hair, caught hold of the bodice of her *gallabeya* at the neck, and split it down the front. A long line of women marched behind her slapping their faces with the palms of their hands, and screaming out loud in a voice that rose to the heavens.

– Yahou – Yahou – Yahoua.

It was as though they were calling on a god named Yahoua.[1] Sheikh Masoud, dressed in a robe made of

[1] Jehovah.

heavy silk, walked up to them with his slow step. Around his head was wound a turban of pure white silk with a fringe of woven red threads which kept lifting in the air. He moved close up to her mother and spoke to her in quiet, dignified tones.

– Your son has gone to his God in the Heavens.

She beat on her naked breast with a hand that was hardened and chapped. She squeezed her black nipple tightly between two fingers, and a stream of milk shot out. She screamed at the top of her voice.

– Son of my womb. Son of my womb.

The women gathered around her screamed in a single voice:

– Son of my womb! Son of my womb!

– Your son is in the Paradise of Eden with the Prophets and the martyrs, said Sheikh Masoud as he stood in front of a row of village guards who had come with him. When he pronounced the word 'martyrs' his neck stretched upwards towards the heavens. He opened his mouth as wide as he could to bring out the word in all the fullness of its meaning. He closed his eyes but his mouth remained open as though he were yawning and falling asleep with the word still not out of his mouth.

Her mother suddenly fell silent. She walked up to him on her big, bare feet. Her breast was naked, exposed, and her eyes were staring. She climbed over him as she would clamber over a cow in the fields, and covered his head in handfuls of dust, raining curses down on him. She cursed his mother and his father, and the father of his father, and the whole of his ancestry, seven generations back. She cursed the Paradise of Eden, and the prophets, and the martyrs and anyone who had anything to do with them. She cursed the Kings and the Pharaohs as far back as the god Ra'a.

The sun was dropping down in the sky ready to set. The children gathered on the river bank to watch. The village guards also followed the scene. Each of them carried a gun with a long bayonet fixed to it. Their eyes were half-closed in sleep. All this went back to the times of Noah, and had been repeated so often that they were tired of seeing it.

Then the words *Village Headman* sounded in the air like shots from a gun. They opened their eyes with a start. It was the first time they had heard a woman curse the Village Headman. She could curse the King, or the Pharoah, or the prophets of God. These were names they read about in books, or sometimes faces pictured in the newspapers. But the Headman of the Village was real. They saw him walking along the river bank, or looking out at them from his house. They heard his voice when he made a speech. He had a prison near the cemetery, and chains, and armed soldiers at his beck and call.

They crowded round her mother. There were twenty of them. Thirty or forty, said the village people later on. They were unable to get a hold on her. When she hit one of them with her fist he fell back down the river bank. They said a spirit called Eblis got into her. The Devil was known in the village since the early days of the first Pharaoh of Egypt. They had seen him walk at night close to the cemetery. He stole into the body of women much more often than men. And when he did that a woman would have the strength of forty men. She could climb over any man, be he the Village Headman himself.

No one came near her any more. They watched her from a distance with frightened eyes, muttered the verse of the Seat under their breath, to chase away the evil spirits and the genii. Her mother walked along the river bank holding her head upright in the air.

– Where is my son, o Zahra? she kept crying out.

The children walked around her repeating what she said in a chorus:

– Where is my son, o Zahra?

She twirled round and round herself like someone dancing. She burst into peals of laughter, laughed so much that there were tears in her eyes. The laughter suddenly stopped in her throat. She dried the tears that flowed as she wept and stared into space.

– O mother of justice and mercy where is my son?

She walked through the narrow lanes on her big, bare feet searching under the piles of refuse and in the heaps of dung.

– Where is my son, o people? she said.

She knocked at doors in the night, and asked:

– Where is my son, Yahoua?

She climbed up the bank of the river and walked. The light of the moon fell on her long dark hair as she advanced close to its waters, and her face was pale and white, without a drop of blood.

The children hid themselves beneath the river bank. The men threw stones at her thinking they were stoning the Devil. But she walked on with her head held up. Behind her she left a trail of blood. She walked on and on without stopping. The stones kept flying at her from every side, but she went on treading squarely on the ground with her bare feet. Her head never bent itself. Blood kept flowing down in a thin stream from her nose and mouth, from her eyes. The sun dropped down behind the horizon but her body stood erect. It seemed to merge with the line where the earth and the sky met, just below her upright head. Her voice kept coming to Nefissa as she lay on the mat near the entrance to the hut. It was like a whispering of the wind and it said:

– Where is your brother, Nefissa?

She dried her eyes with the palm of her hand as she stood behind the window in a robe of white cotton. The female ward was enveloped in darkness. She put her head between the iron bars and took a deep breath, but there was no air. There was only something like a suspended heat loaded with particles of sand. The desert stretched out before her pitch black, like a sea of tar. She could smell burning kerosene, petrol fumes in the air.

Her lips parted and let out one word:

– O God.

He was standing behind the tree-trunk and heard her call out to him. He did not recognise her voice at once. He thought she was the Head Nurse so he hid behind the tall tree-stump. But the voice came to him from the female ward, and he could see the shadow of a woman moving behind the glass of the window. His ears stood erect, trying to catch any sound.

– O God.

Her voice was low, and prolonged itself into a sigh. It resembled Nefissa's voice. He stepped out from behind the tree-trunk into the light. She moved back. He was tall and broad-shouldered and his head was wrapped in a turban like the Headman. His aspect was awe-inspiring like the King or the President. But his feet were unshod. Could he be God? In her dreams she used to see God walking on bare feet like her mother. His feet were big, and he trod on them with all his weight. Behind him followed his shadow. It was long, stretching out over the ground. His footprint showed on the ground like her mother's did. Her eyes followed the track as they went along.

The path between the fields ended at the asphalt road. There his footprints stopped. She looked round and asked:

– Where am I?

They said:

– In Al Kahira.[1]

She said to a man walking on crutches:

– Tell me Uncle. What does *Al Kahira* mean?

– It means a place that oppresses.

– Oh. What's going to be my fate now?

She spat into the open neck of her *gallabeya* and walked on, her eyes wide open, and staring with fright. The asphalt road burnt her feet. All around, leather shoes beat down on the ground. The women's faces were covered in paint but their legs were naked. Horns blew loudly, bells rang and thousands of voices called out from the tops of minarets. Drums beat. Columns of soldiers stamped with their iron-shod heels on the asphalt road. Tanks rolled along with a roar, and the sirens of police cars shrieked.

She looked into the faces of people as she walked. She was searching for her brother's face. All the faces were unknown to her. She could not recognise anyone and no one seemed to know her. She sat down next to a stone fence and leaned her head against it. She might have fallen asleep for a moment. When she

[1] Cairo. The Arabic *Al Kahira* means the triumphant, the oppressor, so powerful as to oppress.

opened her eyes she found a man wearing a white *gallabeya* standing in front of her. Round his waist was a thin belt tied in a bow. His eyes looked familiar. They had the same look as her mother's when she stared into space. This feeling of something she knew attracted her to him. He could be someone from her village who had come to the city. She moved nearer to him and asked:

– Have you seen my brother anywhere, uncle?

– Your brother?

– My brother went to the army and never came back.

– Look for him. You'll find him.

– Where can I look, uncle?

– In the prisons or the Yellow Palace.

He burst out laughing. His laugh was like a thin nervous cough. She hid her face in her hands and started to sob.

– No, uncle, no. Prison is less terrible.

– What is prison? Only fools go to prison. Intelligent people go to the Palace with us.

– Have mercy on us, o God.

She was standing at the window looking out from the female ward. Around her head she had tied a white scarf. Her eyes were wide open, staring. Her lips murmured.

– O God.

Her voice floated through the night like the whisper

of a breeze. The heads of the trees swayed, making dark, moving shadows on the ground.

The echo repeated itself.

– O God.

He moved forwards slowly in the dark, stopped and lifted his eyes up to the window.

– Yes, Nefissa, he said.

His voice resembled her mother's voice when she called out to her. His large head was surrounded by a halo of light. He inspired awe, like a king or the Head-man of the Village. His foot was big, unshod like the foot of the Prophet. He said:

– Nefissa, come down.

She whispered softly in the dark:

– As Thou dost command, o God.

She wound a white veil around her head and tip-toed stealthily out of the female ward, then down the long, dark corridor. Her arms were held out in front of her as though she were walking in her sleep. She went down the stairs and passed through the corridors without being stopped. He took her by the hand and guided her to a hidden corner of the garden. Her eyelids were tightly closed. She did not dare to open them. Sheikh Masoud said that if she opened her eyes she would be struck blind by the powerful light.

– You are a virtuous woman, Nefissa.

– Yes, my God.

– Did the Devil ever whisper anything into your ears?

– No, never, my God.

– Did he ever visit you in the female ward?

– No, never, my God.

– Did you ever come down to meet him here?

– Not once, my God.

– Then bend down and say, I am your obedient slave.

She bent down on her knees and kissed his hand. His hand was broad and white like a pure white comb of honey, and it was as smooth as silk. It was even smoother than the hand of the Village Headman. His nails were clean, carefully clipped. But in his clothes was a smell of sweat. Did God sweat like human beings? Her doubts did not last for more than a moment.

– I am your slave, she said.

She pronounced the word *slave* with a slight hoarseness, a soft crack in her voice. It came out from her parted lips, full of a deep humility and submissiveness. He was standing in the dark, staring at nothing. The tone of her voice caressed his ears, flowed down into his blood like a wave of heat. Here was a real female, not like his wife. She thought she was his equal. He closed his eyes, abandoning himself to the thrill that went through him.

– You shall be my obedient wife, Nefissa.

– At Your feet, my Lord God.

– Am I the first man in your life?

– Yes, my God.

– The only one to whom you owe allegiance?

– The only one, my God.

– No one else, either human, or spirit, Nefissa.

– Neither a human being, nor a spirit. No one apart from you, my Lord.

– I need proof of that, Nefissa.

– As you wish, my Lord.

She did not open her eyes to see what would happen. She felt her *gallabeya* being lifted, his fingers creeping up over her body. The beating beneath her ribs came to a stop. She murmured the opening verse of the Koran.

– He is the one everlasting God.

Then suddenly she felt something searing like a flame. His huge hand was clapped over her mouth preventing her from breathing. She felt she would suffocate. A piercing scream escaped from her lips, splitting the deep silence.

– Yahoua – yahoua.

Whistles shrilled out and the lights came on. The Head Nurse appeared, running, with a whistle in her mouth. Behind her were male nurses carrying ropes.

They tied him up and carried him to the room for electric shocks. Nefissa went on screaming. She could not stop. Her eyes were closed. She could not open them. But her mouth was open and it let out one long, continuous, never-ending scream.

7 *Ganat in a Moment of Consciousness*

She was in her room, lying on her back. She heard the scream. It passed over her closed lids. It resounded in her head, long and never-ending, like the never-ending darkness in which she lived. One scream amidst a million voices, fusing, dissolving into them to become a mighty shout like people demonstrating, so that the million voices became like one continuous, drawn-out scream that died out in the night.

Her ears were strained to hear to their utmost. Her eyes were closed. She heard a prolonged, whistling sound like a violent wind blowing in the distance, or like the echo of a deep silence in the ears. They were all silent, and they were all shouting at the top of their voices, and their voices were like the roar of a waterfall.

– Down with the system. Down! Down!

She opened her mouth and shouted out as loud as she could:

– Down! Down!

The road extended in front of her as far as the

horizon. She was running along it with the boys and girls. Sounds like firing kept coming from behind. Her legs began to falter, to slow down. She felt her body go heavy, and her breath come in gasps. The air was thick with smoke, loaded with defeat like the remains of a huge fire still burning with an odour of petrol fumes. The scattered remains of children floated in the air, like fine ashes or soot, like the first gaseous hazes in the universe which condensed into earth and heaven and planetary bodies. The Khamaseen[1] winds were blowing incessantly enveloping the world in yellow clouds, and fine black drops kept falling like black rain.

– The desert storm.

The words struck on her ears like a sudden blow. The voice kept coming from behind her. She stopped for a moment. Her face looked upwards at the sky and her back was turned to him. She held out her hands to the rain. The heads of the trees shook in the gusts of wind. Their leaves kept dropping on the ground. Her arm was long and thin like a dry wooden stick, and she could see her fingers trembling. There was something in the air, something unknown, fearful. She stretched out her neck and strained her ears to hear.

– Ganat!

Her name rang strangely in her ears, as though this

[1] Hot desert winds that blow over Egypt usually in the late spring and early summer carrying clouds of sand.

was the first time she was hearing it. Who could be calling out to her? Who could know her name amongst the millions of names in the world? She made an effort to open her eyes. Something like a leather belt seemed to be pulled tight around her head. She tried to lift her body up on one elbow. The world seemed to whirl around her, and the voice continued to call out her name. It was a strange voice but it had a familiar hoarseness to it, like the voice of her grandfather who had died, but whose spirit woke up in the night to visit her grandmother. She could hear the sound of his steps on the floor in the hall. He tapped the ground with his stick, and the taps were regular, one tap after the other. She could hear them almost coinciding with the tick of the clock on the wall. She hid her head under the covers as she lay near her grandmother in bed. The steps ceased in front of the door of their room and silence reigned. Now she could hear nothing but the sound of the beats under her ribs, and the breathing of her grandmother as her chest rose and fell. Her eyes were open. They shone in the dark and her eyelashes trembled.

– Why are you awake, Ganat?

– And why are *you* awake, Nena?

Her grandmother gave her a long, slow stare. This girl. She was strange. Whenever she asked her a question she would answer back with a question herself.

– Go to sleep, Ganat.

– Sleep doesn't want to come to me, Nena.

She patted her with her shrunken, blue-veined hand. Her voice echoed softly in her ears, tender like the voice of her mother when she put her to sleep:

– Hou, hou, sleep, sleep, sweet child. Sleep. Hou, hou, sleep, sweet child.

She closed her eyes and slept. The bed creaked. She heard it, half-opened her eyes and peered through them. She could see her grandmother slip out from under the eiderdown. The door opened without a sound and closed again.

She held her breath and strained her ears to hear. Through the closed door came muffled gasping noises like someone trying to conceal laughter or a prolonged sobbing that went on and on. In the morning she would see her grandmother standing at the window clothed in her long black dress with a wide collar of shining beads. The lower part of her legs showed white and fat under the fine black stockings. Her feet looked small in the patent leather shoes with thin, tapering, high heels. She held a Bible in her hands and read from it in a low, whispering voice:

– Our Father which art in Heaven forgive us our trespasses.

Before her grandfather died her grandmother would take off her shoes before praying and read from the Koran instead of the Bible. As soon as they married he started to teach her how to do her ablutions and read from the Koran. But at night she could hear her repeat the name of Jesus Christ under her breath as she hid the Bible under her pillow where nobody would see it.

    – Is the Bible the book of God, Nena?

    – Of course, my child.

    – You mean God has two books like Grandfather?

    – Grandfather! Grandfather what, my child? God is on high above everyone else.

    – Where above everyone else, Nena?

    – In the high Heavens.

    – And what about the Devil, Nena?

    – Go to sleep, child. Enough of your questions.

Her grandmother stared at her out of red-rimmed eyes. The girl was a devil. She was born with her eyes wide open. She slipped out of her mother's belly and stared around her at the world. People were born with their eyes closed and their mouths open ready to scream, but she was born with her eyes open and her mouth tightly shut. When her grandmother saw her she gasped with fright and spat into the neck of her bodice.

    – *I do seek refuge in thee, o God, from the evil of the Devil.*

She made her mother take a bath to wash away the blood and the sin. In the Bible to bear a child was a sin that God only forgave women by making them suffer regret and pain. At night she would glimpse her mother standing at the window. Her eyes were full of pain and bitterness. She would lift her hand up to the stars and cry out:

– O Zahra, mother of justice and mercy.

She sang with her mother in a low voice. She was lying in her arms with her head on her breast. She could hear her sing as she rocked her before she went to sleep:

– Sleep, sweet child, sleep. Hou, hou, sleep, sweet child.

The sound of her cradle as it swayed was like an old melody wafted to her ears. It flowed through her veins with the blood. The heartbeats under her ribs quickened. She made an effort to open her lids and look into her mother's eyes. They were a clear, sheer blue like the colour of the sea. Over their surface was a thin film of tears that made them shine. In front of her lay a sheet of white paper. She was writing on it and her fingers around the pen looked smooth and white, but the letters which moved over the lines were black, dropping down from the pen one after the other, so that the white sheet of paper became crowded with black words, and the pages filled up one after the other, and after a while looked like the pages of the Koran or the Bible, and the letters all looked the same.

Her eyes were wide open in the dark. Was it possible that her mother was able to write? She thought women could not write. Amongst men only her grandfather and God knew how to write.

– Go to sleep, Ganat.

Her grandmother's voice cut through her reverie. She dreamt of writing like her mother. But her grandmother said to her that God had not created women to write, and she read out to her the story of Eve and the serpent from the Bible.

– *Thou shalt crawl on thy belly throughout eternity, and thy longing shall be for thine husband and he shall rule over thee.*

Her grandmother stuck out her tongue between her lips as she pronounced the words. She breathed in gasps as she lay on her brass bed and the four bedposts rattled. Before her grandfather died her grandmother often used to hide the Bible in a box under the bed, and she kept the cross in a red velvet pouch. Yet she kneeled behind him on the prayer carpet and repeated after him:

– *Say God is one and everlasting. He gave birth to no one and was not born himself.*

She choked over the words, swallowed them with her dry saliva, all except the last sentence. It stuck in her throat, protruding like an Adam's apple, rising and falling with her breathing. She drew the sign of the cross on her breast and said:

– The Father, the Son and the Holy Ghost.

– Who's the Holy Ghost, Nena?

– Go to sleep, Ganat.

But she did not go to sleep. She crept out of bed while her grandmother slept, and went on tiptoe to her mother's room. The bed was empty, and papers were strewn over the floor. The light of the moon stole into the room, pallid as the colour of death. The papers shone like silver and the letters on them were black. Her mother's handwriting was fine, exact. She put the dots carefully in place. One word followed the other closely over the lines. The lines were regular. They lay one above the other under the light. She had learnt how to read and could follow the words as they went.

– I do not fear you.

– You who forbid knowledge and snuff out the light.

– You who hide behind the face of God.

– You who sow fear and submission instead of love.

– You who kill thousands of innocent human beings.

– You who have punished me like the serpent, brought down on me an eternal curse.

She lifted her eyes from the paper. He was standing near the water-closet. His shadow lay over the ground, dark and tall. A drop of red blood glimmered on the white tiles. The voice she heard was the voice of her dead grandfather. On his chest lay a golden disc.

– Zakaria?

The name rang in her ears with a familiar sound. She had heard it day after day and year after year. Day after day for thirty years. Her picture in the wedding dress hung on the wall. It was white, the colour of the shroud they wrapped dead bodies in. His face looked out from the picture, stony, unmoving. It was square like the head of Aboul Houl. Around his neck was a black tie like a hangman's cord with a tight bow in front which they called a *papillon*. She continued to run on and on without stopping. The road stretched out before her endlessly, and the night was dark, without moon or stars. Drops of black rain fell from above on the trees and her heartbeats under her ribs echoed the pattering sound they made. The air was heavy, stifling, saturated with smoke, weighed down by defeat. A black mist enveloped the universe with the smell of burning oil. The Khamaseen winds had a distant roaring sound like millions of voices shouting from afar.

– Down! Down!

She could hear her own voice echoing in her ears. Her body jogged up and down with the movement of the car, a long-nosed black limousine. Her fingers holding on to the edge of the window were seized with a fit of trembling. Something hung in the air, unknown, fearful. She stretched her neck and looked out of the window, at her feet racing over the ground in front of the car. She sat on the seat panting for breath, and her hand moved out to feel the gift lying beside her. It was a new bow-tie made of white satin with green spots, and the box was tied in a green ribbon. She wound down the window, breathing in the smells of home-coming after two weeks abroad. They had seemed to her like two years, or two centuries, so she cut short her trip and came back three days early. Her breathing grew faster the closer she got, and the beating beneath her ribs rushed forward with the movement of the tyres over the road. Her eyes kept seeing her home, her mother and her father, the ears of corn and the cotton blossoms dancing in the fields. University Street and the college buildings, and his voice. It came from above her, from the platform as he spoke. And thousands of voices chanted in unison:

– Long live! Long live!

Her eyes looked into his eyes for a long moment. They were sitting in the gardens of Andalusia[I] and he was holding her hand between his with a gentle pres-sure.

– Ganat.

– Yes?

– Are you dreaming?

– Yes.

He smiled happily. No doubt she was dreaming of him.

– What are you dreaming of, my darling?

– I want to write.

The smile froze on his face.

[I] The name of a garden in Cairo near the Nile.

– What is it you want to write, Ganat?

– A lot of things.

– Write me a love letter.

At night she sat in the moonlight and wrote him her first letter.

– I love you as I love the forbidden fruit.

On the tree of knowledge.

I stretch out my hand and pluck it off.

I am not afraid

For God is love.

She half-opened her eyes. Her head shook with the movement of the car. The disc of the sun slid down behind the pyramids. The driver of the car was wearing a military cap. The smell of home was in her nose along with particles of dust and shaving cream and aftershave lotion with the scent of lavender. His breath on her face had a special smell which kept coming to her. She looked around for it under the roof of the car. It preceded him, and stayed with her after he left. She buried her face in his breast and gasped out.

– Zakaria.

The car stopped in front of the house. Her feet flew up the stairs faster than herself. She stopped in front of the door, panting, hesitating as though afraid to go in. She put her bag on the floor, and took the key out of her pocket. Should she open the door or should she ring the bell?

She opened the door without a sound and tiptoed in, holding her breath. She wanted to surprise him. She wanted him to look up suddenly and find her there in front of him. She wanted to watch his eyes as they filled with light, to hold him in her arms all night. In the morning she would open the box and take out the present she had bought for him.

The key slipped into the keyhole and turned without making a sound. The hall was enveloped in darkness. A faint light filtered through from the bedroom. The door was slightly open and she could hear music.

She stood behind the door breathing deeply. Her breath was coming in gasps, out of control as though some other mind felt what she could not feel. Her grandmother called it the 'inner mind'.

Her scream pierced through the night, shrill and prolonged. It was the scream of her mother and of her grandmother before her. The same scream. A single, long scream that went on interminably in her ears, like water dropping down a waterfall. Like the millions of voices which created the silence of the night. Everyone was dead and everyone was shouting.

– Down! Down! Fallen! Fallen!

She turned over in the bed, opened her eyes. She glimpsed her grandmother's body standing upright draped in a long dress of black muslin. Her hair was tied with a wide, black, satin cloth which she called a turban. Dark blue, swollen veins showed under the skin of her fat white legs. In her hand she carried her shoes made of shiny patent leather with long, tapering heels. She waved her shoes in the air and shrieked.

– Fallen! Low!

– A man only falls in elections, my lady.

Her grandfather nodded his head affirmatively. He was sitting dressed in his military uniform with a medal pinned to his chest. His face was square like Zakaria's, and white as a sheet. His hair had fallen from his head except above the ears leaving a few white strands that waved like feathers. He stretched his neck forwards like a turkey cock.

– Only a woman can be said to have fallen, my lady.

He nodded his head again. The strands above his ears moved in the air. He pulled at them with his fingers to hide his bald head. There were a number of men sitting round a marble table. Their faces were familiar to her. She had seen them often since the day she was born, or maybe before that in another life. Among them was her grandfather with his huge hooked nose which made him resemble an eagle or a hawk. It was the sign that he was really his father's son, that he was born of his loins.

– Yahoua, Yahoua.

A voice like her mother's voice was screaming in the silence. It was a scream that went on and on, interminable as the night. It was the scream that her grandmother let out as though she were turning to a

God called Yahoua, asking him to come to her help, to save her, to witness her state. He was the god of volcanoes and earthquakes, of the catastrophes which befell the earth. He never came, never answered her call. Instead he sent the spirit of her dead grandfather, the one who stood near the door of the water-closet with a black pipe between his lips. It had a long cob like a trumpet which curved forwards and resembled the antlers of a deer. From his nostrils he expelled two columns of smoke which rose up to the ceiling. They filled the air with a dark mist heavy with smoke, and loaded with the weight of defeat. The Khamaseen winds continued to whistle and she ran on without stopping. His voice followed on her heels. It resembled the voice of Zakaria and kept shouting:

– Fallen! You whore!

His voice was hoarse and cracked and his tongue protruded from his lips as he panted behind her. He opened his jaws to the utmost when he shouted the words, like someone yawning, then he clenched his teeth.

She was still running with her back to him and her face to the horizon. Her feet sounded on the ground and under her ribs her heart echoed the rhythm of her feet. She rushed out of the bedroom, crossed the corridor in one leap, and ran down the stairs not caring whether she fell. She opened the door of the garage with a single push of her hand. It had never opened like that before. She awakened the engine of the car with a quick pressure of her foot. It had never responded before without at least three or four attempts. The Fiat reversed through the door of the garage without grazing anything. She had never been able to bring it out without hitting the wall or the door at least once.

The white-bodied Fiat went through space like a silver fish. Her hands turned the steering wheel to the right and to the left. Her heart was beating under her ribs with a sound like voices which kept clamouring:

– Down! Down! Fallen! Fallen!

The sound of car horns mingled with the screech of trains on their rails, the wailing accompanying the dead to their burial, the 'you-yous' of a wedding celebration, the bells of churches, the calls to prayer rising from a thousand minarets, the entreaties of beggars, and the cries of newspaper vendors, the music of military marches and the blaring microphones of election campaigns and the roar of tanks rolling through the streets. But above all she could hear the sound of the engine rising higher than any sound she had ever heard before, like the sound of a million voices crying out:

– Fallen! Fallen! Low! Low!

The four wheels seemed like wings flying over the ground. Her black hair blew around her head. She could see her eyes in the mirror of the car. Thirty years of sadness, thirty years. Under the surface was a gleam like a ray of light, like the eyes of another woman being born, happy to be saved. She lifted her hands from the wheel and clapped them together with the glee of a child set free. The beat of her heart danced under her ribs and the car danced along the road to the same beat. She hugged the steering wheel as though she were hugging her mother close to her heart.

– Ganat.

She woke up with a start, opened her eyes to the drab white surface of the cracked ceiling. In front of her stood a woman dressed in a white uniform. Her head was swathed in a veil. Its colour was grey. Over her breast shone a golden disc. On it was a square face with the beak of an eagle.

– Zakaria?

– I am the Head Nurse.

The Head Nurse shook her head from side to side with a movement which was meant to indicate no, and came closer with the syringe she was holding in her hand. She rubbed her arm with a piece of cotton wool, and the smell of alcohol went up her nose. Their eyes met in a steady gaze. The Head Nurse's eyes seemed familiar, something in their expression, in the outer film of sadness, with the child underneath looking out.

– Narguiss?

– I am the Head Nurse.

And she shook her head again to say no. She took hold of her arm ready to plunge the needle into her flesh, but she knocked her hand away. The syringe flew out of it and broke into pieces on the ground.

– I won't take the injection!

– You must!

– I won't!

She hit the table with her fist and it split in two. In the mouth of the Head Nurse the whistle blew, long and persistent like the whistle of the wind, yet halting and hesitant like a sobbing voice. The male nurses appeared wearing white aprons. There were three or four of them, and maybe more. They tried to sieze hold of her but failed. Then they tried to lift her up and carry her to the electric shock room. Her body could not be separated from the bed, or shifted to the trolley. They tried again and again. Her body would not move. It was as though it had become one with what was around it, with the ground, with the earth, with the bed on which she lay, and no one could detach her from her place.

More male nurses came in, ten, twenty, even thirty, but to no avail. Her body and the bed and the ground were a single mass which refused to yield, as though her soul had come back to her body, and no one could separate them again.

The eyes of the male nurses were wide open and full of fear. They shouted out in one voice.

– The Devil has taken over her body.

The whistle blew. It was like an unending scream that lasted all through the night.

8 *Guilt*

She was running down the corridor with the whistle between her lips. Her feet were inside a pair of rubber shoes and her head was enveloped in a veil. The golden disc trembled over her breast and her body was shaking as she ran.

She entered her room and closed the door behind her. She rested her head against it and stood panting. The whistle fell from her lips. She held it in one hand and crushed it between her fingers. Her other hand lay on her chest. It touched the golden disc, crept under her white uniform to her left breast, then further down her ribs. There she could feel it under her hand, round like a swelling, hiding behind the wall of her heart where it had accumulated year after year for thirty years.

Her fingers were ashen grey and they were trembling. From the moment the huge gate had opened, and she had walked in, her heart had started to beat in a different way. She could feel it. She was sitting in the Director's room when she saw her walk in. Suddenly a cloud descended over her eyes, and the sky filled with a grey mist. From behind the glass she could see the Director's face. It had become as white as chalk. His hair started to fall off his head, and the plaster on the walls started to fall off too. The leaves were falling off the trees and the wind was whistling in the distance.

– Yahou – yahou – yahou.

The whistling echoed in her ears like a million voices. Then the sound faded away gradually until it became a soft tune like the whispering of the wind when it moved the heads of the trees, and the long wires stretched out above the high wall of the fence. The echo kept repeating itself in different parts of the palace as it passed through the cracks in the walls, or along the corridors and distant passages. Ears strained to hear from behind closed doors as it came to them. Eyes remained open all night behind windows covered with iron bars. Through each square an eye looked out like a flaming star, like an eye filling up with light at the moment of death, as the mind lights up with understanding just before it is switched off forever inside the head.

– Yahou. Yahou. Yahou.

The sound repeated itself like a thousand chests breathing deeply in sleep. It crossed over the wall and moved through the city. The city was called El Kahira from the verb *kahara* in the past, and *yakhar* in the present which means oppress. But El Kahira did not oppress. It was the city of the oppressed. Its people walked the streets with long, pallid faces. Their eyes were half-closed, their mouths half-open. They looked at the palace from a distance and made the sign of the cross, or the crescent. They prayed to God to protect them from the Devil. The palace filled their hearts with the fear they had for devils and spirits, and for the ancient gods going back as far as the time of Noah. During the day it was yellow like the heavy Khamaseen winds. At night it became a black mass within which moved white shapes. They looked out of dark squares, or floated along like aimless spirits in the bare dry grounds around the palace called the garden where grew a few wild, thorny plants and tufts of grass. Here and there were stone columns with pharaonic inscriptions. The names of the god Ra'a and the Calf of Ibis. There were ancient trees, a thousand years old or more. No one could tell their exact age. The trunks rose high up into the sky or were stumps with their heads cut off. The bark was black with ragged cracks like deep wrinkles that sank into the trunk down to its marrow.

Time was so old that it seemed to stand still. Silence was total except for a faint whisper, the whisper of the wind. A sustained, faint whistle, so long-drawn out that it extended as far as the horizon. The million voices that made up the silence of the night.

– Yahou – yahou – yahou.

She strained her ears as she stood close to her window right at the top. It was without iron bars for she was the Head Nurse. The breeze came to her from the northern balcony. Over the window was a fine lace curtain, worked by hand. Her bed had brass posts, and was covered with a red satin eiderdown. On the wall hung her picture in a golden frame. It showed her receiving the decoration. She stood on a step bending downwards from the waist. Her right hand stretched out with open fingers. It was stretched out as far as it could reach and she was bent over at the waist, so that her head almost hit against the wooden platform. But although her arm was long, it could not cross the distance no matter how far she stretched. The distance was made of wood and on the wood were rows of medals. She made a last effort, stretched out her neck, and bent forward with her body as far as she could. Her head hit up against the platform. Now she could take hold of the medal with her right hand. She moved out her left hand, but remembered suddenly that people did not shake hands with the left. On the Day of Judgement people would shake God's hand with their right hand, not with the left. That's what her grandfather had said. Paradise would be on the right of the straight path to God. And Hell would be on the left. The Devil also always stood on the left.

Her hand was seized with a violent trembling. She

thought they might take back the medal because she had reached out with her left hand. Before anyone could notice she shifted the medal to the other hand, and stretched out her right arm as far as she could towards the platform.

At night when she dreamt, the handshake of that day came back. It was not a complete handshake. The hand from the platform did not have five fingers. Or perhaps the fingers were stuck to one another inside a glove as tight as a skin. Also the hand had taken refuge inside the arm, and the arm was stuck to the chest. The chest was broad and solid, encased in an iron shield. Upon it were shining medals, and decorations, and from it rose a neck which curved upwards like that of a turkey cock. At the top of the neck was a square face. It was grey in colour like the stone of the Mokattam Hills, and was held up in the air without moving like the head of Aboul Houl.

His hand never moved beyond the edge of the platform. It was not supposed to stretch out more than a short distance, calculated to the millimetre. It was the other hand that was expected to move over the remaining distance. To do that it had to take the whole length of the arm with it, and with the arm the neck, and with the neck the trunk, which had to bend forwards at an angle. Only then could the tips of her fingers touch the tips of his fingers quickly, like a flash of lightning, or an electric shock. For at this precise moment the flashlights would settle on her, and her picture would appear in the newspapers. Her face would show white, as white as the magnesium flare in the flash. Her teeth would be bared and white too, showing in a smile, a broad opening-up of the mouth which was twisted to one side.

Ever since the days of the god Ra'a the ruler had always stood on this platform. He would look out of the corner of his eye at something, and the spirit would descend upon him. The wooden stick would then become a snake, which would start moving around or would change into a lizard. When the ruler was a King or a President it was sufficient for the tip of his finger to touch the hand of a woman from among the common people for her to become a Head Nurse, or if it were a man for him to become a Director or a Cabinet Minister. His name would be inscribed in the annals on a stone column, or on something else. They would engrave his three names[1] on a plate made of gold, or silver, or bronze, or copper according to his status, his family, and his ancestral tree. Then the metal disc would be pinned to his chest.

It was a mark of status that went back in history as far as the Ibis calf. The platform was made from the trunk of a tree with its head cut off. The heads were the same heads. They looked like sons of Adam and

[1] The first name, the father's first name, and the surname, required for accurate identification on official papers.

daughters of Eve. Their trunks had to bend in the same way at the waist, and the right knee had to bend at the same time as the neck. He would be standing inside the clothes of His Majesty or His Excellency, or His Honour. The head was the same head. It was square and the colour of white granite. At the top it ended in a pyramidal shape with a feather coming out of it, or strands of hair that floated in the wind, and the wind blew with a sound like whistling in the distance.

– Yahou. Yahou.

She was still standing, her eyes fixed on the picture hanging on the wall. The whistle had fallen from her mouth. It lay on her breast and kept moving up and down with it. Her fingers felt the inscriptions on the golden disc. Its surface was smooth, and on it were engraved her three names. She could feel their letters stand out and hear the voice of the Director loud in her ears:

– The Medal of Honour for exemplary fulfillment of duty and for bringing happiness to others.

The palm of her hand was moist with sweat. Her eyes swept round the walls which showed cracks and dark lines. The ceiling was drab, and its plaster had fallen off in some places. The fallen pieces had left shapes which resembled a head with a horn curving to the front. A yellow electric lamp hung from a long yellow wire. A dead fly was stuck to the wire, and refused to fall off.

She stretched her moist hand out through the open window. Blue swollen veins showed beneath the wrinkled skin. It resembled the hand of her grandmother. Her voice whispered in a hiss:

– Able to make others happy but incapable of bringing happiness to herself?

Her chest rose and fell as she stood at the window, as though she were out of breath from running. From behind the closed door she could hear the voice. It was like someone weeping silently, or gasping, or making a long sighing sound that went on and on all through the night.

– Naaarguiss! Naaarguiss!

The voice went through her. It was like the voice of her mother when she called out to her, or the voice of her dead grandmother, or like that of any other woman, a relation of hers, or a neighbour, or one of her colleagues in school. The night was silent. The wind carried the voice. It called out to her across the distances like a sad, lonely flute. She could hear it as she lay curled up in her bed, like a child in its mother's womb, under the cotton eiderdown which covered her body from head to foot. She was afraid to show her head above the covers. He was there standing behind the clothes-stand, tall, broad, his hand holding the door. He was wearing the robe of her dead grandfather, and her father's red *fez*. His head was big and square, like that of the Director, his neck long, stretching

upwards like a turkey cock. In his hand he carried the
stick of Sheikh Bassiouni. It writhed in the air like a
snake. He was disguised in a bridegroom's clothes, in
a black jacket and a tie which encircled his neck below
the chin. It was knotted in a bow which they called a
papillon. Between his lips dangled a black pipe which
curved forwards like the horn of the Ibis calf, or the
trunk of an elephant.

She knew he was no more than a spirit or a genie.
She believed in spirits and genii. They were mentioned
in the book. He hid when she put on the lamp, but
she was afraid to put her hand out from under the
covers, and she dared not go to the water-closet, or
the House of Good Manners. He usually settled down
there. She held back the urine in her body all night.
Her *hidden mind*[1] was vigilant and she never wet her
bed even when she slept.

In the morning she put on her school uniform. Her
hidden mind went to sleep when she walked and her
visible mind[2] became separated from her body. She
held her school satchel under her arm. Her feet were
shod in a pair of black shoes fastened with a strap and
a white button. The button kept slipping out of the
buttonhole when she walked. The palm of her hand
was moist with sweat, and she was afraid to open her
fingers. She was also afraid to stretch her legs too wide

[1] Unconscious.
[2] Conscious mind.

apart when she walked. Between her self and her body was a barrier, like a sheet of glass. When people passed her in the street they stopped to look at her. It was as though they were looking at her through the sheet of glass. She could see them peering at her with narrowed, half-open eyes. The surface of her eyes was covered with a film of water and the world seemed to waver behind it as though in a dream. She carried a body which was unreal, and she tried to hide it from people's eyes.

But the eyes were capable of penetrating through the glass. They could follow every movement made by the organs buried in her flesh, for her flesh was thin and as transparent as glass. It permitted light to pass through it, but not air. She held her neck up in a way which people thought was a sign of conceit. In fact she was suffocating and was just trying to get some air for herself.

It was a long distance to school. She walked with a swinging movement of her tall, slim body. She avoided lifting her shoulders lest she become taller than the men. She walked over the soil of her land with a light step. She did not want to tread more heavily than she should. It would mean that she did not love her land enough. Around her neck hung the picture of the King, or the President, or the headmaster of the school. Or perhaps just letters inscribed in Koufie[1] handwriting

[1] A special and particularly decorative way of writing the letters of the Arabic language which comes from Koufa (Iraq).

which said Allah. The picture shook over her breasts as she walked. Her body bent forward as though preparing to escape. Her arms swung forwards and backwards, and the tips of her fingers touched the sides of her buttocks as she walked. She felt like hiding before anyone could get a glimpse of her. If anyone did happen to spot her she shook her head several times as though apologising for being in the world. She smiled timidly to excuse herself for a situation which had been forced upon her, for her body, which should have been invisible, or been just an immaterial spirit without flesh and so able to move over the ground without being touched.

She wanted to walk, to be able to see others without being seen herself. She wanted to fly up to the Heavens, to be able to see God and yet be invisible to Him. No human being could see God face to face. That was what her father had said. One of the prophets, perhaps Abraham or Moses, had dared to look at God. The light had hit him like an electric shock, and he had fallen to the ground almost dead. His teeth kept chattering against one another, as though with fever.

She wanted to see God without being exposed to such shocks, without her teeth chattering like that. She wanted to hear a voice other than that of the Devil. He kept whispering to her at night. She hid her head under the covers, and pressed the pillow down on her head, muttering the words of the Seat. She begged

God to come to her rescue, but He left her to face the Devil all alone. His voice echoed in her ears in the dark, in a whisper which lasted as long as the longest night. It came to her ears soft and tender, like the voice of her mother, and flowed in through her veins like warm blood. Nothing could save her from the Devil except sleep.

In the morning when she walked she hid her breasts behind her school satchel. People's eyes opened wide when they saw her, as though they had seen the Devil whispering to her at night, as though she had no right to be walking in the street, as though they owned the street, and she owned nothing at all. Even the pavement was theirs. She had no share in anything, no share in her land. Not even an inch of it. She had no property, no house. Her father owned nothing. All he had was her, her mother, and his government pension which permitted him to buy bread, but nothing to go with it. She smiled shamefacedly in apology for her poverty, her father's poverty, and her grandfather's poverty. But suddenly she would lift her head with pride. She remembered that she owned a place in Paradise and that since this was the case she could treat the property people owned in the world with disdain.

She trod firmly on the ground as she walked and people looked at her with wide-open, staring eyes, as though she should not tread on the soil of the land with her shoes like that. She bent her head in shame several times as though refuting any possibility that she might be a traitor to her land. When she lifted her head again she found them still staring at her, their eyes fixed on her body as though it were different from the other bodies and belonged to a mammalian species with breasts.

She would whisper to herself:

– I am a human being like the rest of you.

Then she would walk on swallowing her tears. She would stop for a moment if she saw a child crying or a cat mewing, or a beggar walking on crutches. She shared the pain of others. The moment she did that her body put a distance between itself and them, escaped back into her total loneliness and despair with life. But suddenly despair would change into hope for no reason at all, or for very simple reasons like the laughter she caught in the eye of a child as she walked along, or a small puppy shaking its tail as though happy with her presence. Something would shine in her eyes. She could see it in the mirror. It was as real as the sun, creeping out from behind the clouds. She would put out her hand to touch it, but the mirror told her it was not real, and her heart would grow heavy again. She could feel it under her left breast like a swelling, like an old guilt accumulated since the days of Eve and the serpent. God had listened to what Adam had to say and had forgiven him alone. That was what her father had explained to her mother. The verse which came down from God used the singular, not the dual.[1] In the verse concerning the *disobedience*, however, God used the dual form in place of the singular. God had a deep knowledge of language and its rules. He would never use the singular or the dual except in the right context. Her father repeated the words of God in a solemn voice:

– *And we said, Adam thou shalt dwell, thee and thy wife, in Paradise. Neither of you shall go near to this tree. But the Devil led them both to slip into wrongdoing, and so we ordained that they descend from here and be to one another as enemies.*

Her father emphasised the word *enemies* and stared at her mother with bloodshot eyes. He repeated the phrase *both to slip* three times, expelling the word *both* from his lips with force, and pouting them when he pronounced the *p* at the end of *slip*. Then in sharp tones he recited:

– *God listened to Adam's words and forgave him.*

The word *him* shot out from his mouth with a long, humming sound, emphasising the singular. It was Adam alone who was forgiven.

She could see her mother standing at the window, gazing at the heavens. In her eye hung a tear that never dropped out nor dried. The darkness was endless, and the sky was pitch black with no moon or stars. Only

---

[1] In Arabic words can indicate not only the singular and the plural but also the dual (two).

one star hung in space somewhere between the earth and the heavens, trembling over their heads like a sin that could never be washed away. Its name was Zahra and it burned with a never-ending fire. Her father pointed it out with his long sharp finger and said:

– The whore. She tempted Harout and Marout into sin.

She understood that the curse included her. She repeated the two names Harout and Marout, and felt hot air come out of her mouth as though she were cursing them too. She closed her lips tightly, holding the air back in her chest. Guilt grew under her ribs like a swelling in her flesh. She had to live this sin. No atonement could be made, no words of forgiveness could come from God. She carried her body around her soul like a weight. In her mind it was sometimes an illusion, sometimes a truth. She could never see herself except in the mirror, or in the glass of a door or window, or reflected in a river or stream. She lived in a world unknown to her, in a body which she did not own. It belonged to her father, or to the government, or to her dead grandfather, or to another man, whose features were strange to her, and whose name she had forgotten. He held her in the picture, with one hand and with the other hand he clutched a dead rose.

In the mirror her body looked slim. She carried it like a gift from God, a gift He had taken away from her the minute she was born. She ate little so that her body would be like a spirit without flesh, so that it stayed small, and did not grow to the age of adolescence which made young people irresponsible, or the age of puberty which would make her womb swell with blood.

The word *menses* rang in her ears for the first time as she sat behind her desk in class. Sheikh Bassiouni pouted his lips with disgust as he pronounced the word, and said it was an unholiness from the Devil. The *m* came out of his lips like a pellet of dirt, and the *s* was pronounced with the hiss of a snake. It was like the meat of dead carcasses, and pigs [1] and blood. He stretched out his neck and his nostrils flared. His head passed down the rows of girls like the head of a dog seeking out a smell. Suddenly he stopped at her desk, pulled the Koran out of her hands, [2] and wiped its cover with a piece of cotton moistened with disinfectant.

Her grandmother called it *impurity*. She went into the bathroom with her and washed her down with a rough sponge and soap, all the while repeating the opening verse of the Koran. She recited the testimonial to God and His prophet three times. She chased away the Devil with mugs of hot water poured one after the other over her head. She would cry out behind the

[1] Forbidden to both Muslims and Jews.
[2] Women are supposed to be impure during their periods.

locked door for her mother to come to her rescue. Her mother never came. Her mother called it the *bad blood* or the *monthly sickness*. She gave her half a dozen napkins made out of coarse cotton with a thin strap attached at either end to tie round her waist.

As she walked to school she could feel the napkin between her legs. It rolled itself up like a swelling, like a sin hanging down under her belly. It would slip back over her buttocks. When she sat down she could feel it in the space between her back and the desk. If she moved blood flowed down over her skin, feeling like hot air.

The bell rang at the end of the lesson.

She remained seated in her place, afraid to stand up, for as soon as she did she could feel something like a warm thread run down her leg. It was as smooth as the tail of a snake. It would disappear into her shoe, and wet her socks with a fluid the colour of red ink. She looked around her and as soon as there was no one in sight she walked out cautiously, hugging the wall and hiding her uniform at the back with her satchel. At home she bent over the wash-basin in the water-closet, and washed her uniform and knickers over and over again. But the stain never seemed to disappear, and the sin was never washed away, even if her fingers became swollen and red from rubbing. She would roll up her knickers in a ball and kick them behind her as though they were the evidence of her sin. She was afraid to hang them on the clothes-line lest someone should see them as they flapped in the wind. Instead she dug a pit, and buried them under the earth, like a corpse. Then she hid in her room under the covers as though she had committed a crime, hugging her pillow in her arms and singing to it.

– Hou, hou. Sleep my child, sleep.

The voice of her grandmother wafted to her ears as she sang to her grandchild lying on her lap. Her grandchild was not yet dead. Nevertheless she knew without a doubt that the child was dead, and that she herself was this child. She could hear her voice like the whisper of the wind rustling in the branches of the palm trees. She closed her eyes. Being dead was a pleasurable feeling. People were left alone when they were dead. They did not have to answer questions, or say anything.

She hated talking. She hid in her room so that people would leave her to herself. No one would demand anything from her, or ask her a question. Her body trembled when her mother came into the bathroom with her. She searched in her body for what was considered the most precious thing in a girl. It was something invisible, hidden below the belly. Like a fine sheet of paper that could be torn by a waft of air. Glass could break under the slightest blow, and this fine sheet could tear if she stamped her foot on the stairs. It burned like the head of a match at the slightest friction. People said that was the end, from where there was no return.

Her grandmother pouted her lips when she said 'no return', then closed her eyes and fell asleep. Narguiss stood at the window in the darkness. From beneath the door of the kitchen crept a yellow light. She could hear the sound of water dripping from the tap, and plates knocking against each other in the sink. Her mother's slippers moved over the tiled floor with a stealthy sound, and the noise of the street could be heard from afar. Pale yellow lights crept over the walls. A car passed along in front of the house, its headlights dousing everything in their glare. But later nothing remained except a small circle like a yellow eye which ran over the ceiling and then down to the floor before disappearing.

She could only tell that it was late at night when the sound of plates being washed could no longer be heard. When the tap was turned off and the lights extinguished in the kitchen and in the houses on the street. No light remained on except for a small yellow wick that trembled in the night. Her eyes drowned in an ocean of darkness. They tried to hold on to the smallest ray of light. A single lone star, or a lamp in a small boat crossing an invisible sea. Sadness would envelop her suddenly like a cold cloud. A shiver went through her body and her will to live seemed to be lost like a flame snuffed out by the wind. She stared at the face of the night, or maybe at faces that moved through the night, at the leaves trembling in the wind. She stretched her hand out of the window, as though trying to relate to the world again, or as though looking for something to hold on to in the wide universe. A face, or eyes, or two arms held out to her. At the very moment in which she made this silent gesture and reached out into the darkness, something happened. It was as though she were suddenly rid of all sin, all guilt. Sadness seemed to flow out of her body from every pore. Harmony reigned over her once more, and her soul revived in her body.

Her heart filled up with a strange tenderness, like an overwhelming love. She could see her only friend coming towards her, wearing the same coloured uniform she wore, made of white cotton with blue squares, and with a white collar round the neck. In her hand she carried her satchel of books. She threw it into the air and caught it again with both hands as it fell. She was tall and graceful, her back straight. Her eyes glowed with light. She almost jumped out of the window to embrace her. A cry of joy rose in her throat. She sat her down in her room, and closed the door. Her lips opened to let out a flow of words. Her mother put her ear to the door, trying to pick up what they said. She could only hear sounds emitted like gasps, or bursts of delighted laughter choked back so that they sounded like sobs.

– G, G, G, G, G, Ganat!

– Nar, Nar, Nar, Nar, Nar, Narguiss!

Her name Narguiss rang out in her friend's voice. It had a ring that lived on in the ear, different from any other sound, like small circles of silver light. It dropped through the air like clear water flowing down rocks into the valley. Her friend's skin was dark, the colour of silt. It shone under the sun like burnished copper.

In the mirror she could see her own skin. It was dark too, but it had no lustre, as though its shine had gone. Her friend seemed to be the original and she just a copy, her dark shadow moving behind her through life. A faint, weak carbon copy. Her hands were big. She hid them in the pockets of her uniform. Her feet were bigger than the feet of the Prophet. That was what her grandmother said to her. She hid them under her desk when she sat in class. Her features were hidden under a coating like white flour. Her mother bought it from the chemist packed in a box; it was called powder. Her mother said that a dark complexion was a sign of ugliness, or poverty, or of a slave ancestry, whereas a fair complexion indicated nobility and a fine heritage from a family of masters and dignitaries or even from the King whose ancestry went back to the Prophet Mohammed, God's blessings and peace be on him.

She slept curled up under the covers to hide her

face from prying eyes. In her dreams the Prophet appeared with a fair complexion like that of a king. She had never dreamt of a black prophet, and in her sleep she saw God with a face as white as milk, but the Devil always had a dark complexion. It was so dark that it was almost the same colour as her own.

Her friend did not have white skin. As a matter of fact her skin was also dark. But she walked with her head held high as though she were the daughter of the King. Her hair was thick and black. It flew around her head, and she tossed it back with her hand as only a rebellious mare whom no one owned could do. On the day of the feast she wore an orange-coloured dress which filled up with air, and the pleats flew around her like the wings of a butterfly.

Under her ribs she could feel the beating of her heart. Deep down inside her was a melody which throbbed like a rhythmic dance. The ears of corn in the fields danced under the sun with the same rhythm, and the rustle of the leaves in the wind seemed to whisper the same melody. She stood at the window, poised to leap out and run towards her friend, hold her in her arms, and hug her closely. Their bodies would fuse into one another, and she and her friend would become as one, so that her name Narguiss would no longer exist.

When her mother noticed tears in her eyes she would say to her:

– Narguiss is the name of a beautiful flower.

She would answer:

– But mother, the name Ganat is more beautiful. It is the plural of *Gana*. It means many Paradises, not just one. So how can you compare one lonely flower like Narguiss to it?

A feeling like that of being an orphan filled her heart as she stood at the window, waiting for her friend to come. It was as though she had been born of an unknown father and an unknown mother, as though the land in which she lived was not her land. She lived for that one moment when she and her friend became one. Her love was so deep that it filled her with hope, filled her with the fear that one day she would see her no more, that one day she might hold out her hand to her only to discover that she had disappeared into the air, or been run over by a car or a tram.

When she saw her friend approaching she was afraid that she might turn into someone other than Ganat. She would step backwards, holding her arms up in the air to avoid the embrace, her throat would become dry, and the words would freeze on her lips. The silence would last one or two moments until the fact that it was really her chased away the momentary illusion which held her in its grip. Her tongue would unknot itself and words would flow out. Her mother often asked her what she, the ever-silent girl, could possibly be saying to her friend. At home it was as though her tongue had been cut off yet here she never stopped talking. She did not know what to reply. She did not feel she was saying anything. It was not the words. They were just cooing noises, like those made by doves. A dove would bring its beak close to that of the other dove and the whispering would go on.

She knew how to understand the language of doves even though she had not yet learnt to write. She drew the sounds on the ground with her feet in crooked lines, but her friend could read the letters. She knew the secrets of pigeons and doves, of birds of paradise and of butterflies. She ran after butterflies in the fields, and caught them between her fingers. She brought them close to her mouth and whispered to them. Then she would let them fly up in the air, and clap their wings as they rose up in the sky.

Her mother did not believe what her friend said about the language of birds, and she stopped her from going to her friend's house. When her friend came to their house she sat with them in the room, or put her ear to the door and tried to hear what they were saying. When she slept, she would dream of school where she could meet her friend in the yard. They would jump about like butterflies as they played hopscotch or raced one another. They would skip, and gasp, and laugh, and scream, and stamp up over the stairs, and in the joy of being together they would forget what was the most precious possession of a girl.

In the reading lesson when the teacher asked her who was the person she loved most she did not say, my father, or my mother. She said Ganat. The teacher gave her a zero for manners, and Ganat got a zero also because she liked birds more than her father and mother. A rumour went round the school about a kind of love which the Devil was trying to make appealing to the hearts of the girls. The idea came to her that a struggle was going on between God and the Devil over the young girls' hearts. At night the Devil used to whisper in her ear with a soft voice:

– Love is beautiful.

In the class on religion Sheikh Bassiouni told her to hold out her arms and he beat her fingers with the cane three times, then made her repeat after him nine times:

– God Almighty, I seek Thy mercy for every great sin I have committed.

Ever since she had learnt to pronounce words she had been asking God's forgiveness for the great sins she had committed. Her body could understand this but not her mind. She could feel sin under her fingers like a swelling growing beneath her ribs, and rushing through her veins like hot blood. Or like a match buried in the folds of her flesh, a match which the barber cut off with his razor,[1] so that the sheet was soaked with

---

[1] Clitoridectomy.

blood. She knew it was a sin which hung forever from the high heavens over her head or that it was a shame, a dishonour that could only be washed off by blood.

She stood at the window and asked her mother the reason why. Her mother held her head up. Her eyes were fastened on a small trembling spot of light. A single lonely star, its light cutting through the ocean of night. One tiny drop of light in the vast darkness, hanging somewhere on the horizon between heaven and earth. Always there, fixed, steady, never failing or burning out, never falling from where it hung on high. She would lift her arms and sob in a voice that was like a song, or like a long never-ending plaint stretching through the length of the night.

– O God.

9 *And in the Beginning was the Serpent*

The call floated through the dark spaces around the palace like the whispering of the wind. The trees threw their shadows on the ground. They moved like ghosts, swaying in a lazy movement as though overcome by an extreme state of boredom. He hid behind the tree-trunk, squatting crosslegged on the ground in his white *gallabeya*. His head was covered in the white turban with the feather coming out of the top like a needle. He kept digging in the ground with his big fingers, and the moonlight fell on his face as he dug. His long white beard fell over his chest and his thick eyebrows met over the bridge of his noise. His small, round eyes followed his own fingers closely as they moved over the ground.

– O God.

His ears pricked up as he heard the voice and his fingers ceased their restless search. His lips parted and he whispered softly:

– Who's calling me?

A deep silence reigned all around. No sound could be heard except the rustle of the wind in the trees. He stuck his head out from behind the tree-trunk and glimpsed a faint light in the window. A white shadow was coming and going behind the glass. Her breasts showed white and round under the light of the moon. Her long black hair fell down over her back. Her eyes were closed, and her arms were held out in front of her as though she were walking in her sleep.

– O God.

He slipped out from behind the tree-trunk. The shadow of his tall body lay on the ground, long and dark.

– I am here. I . . .

His voice sounded strange to his ears as though it belonged to another man. It echoed in the silence of the night.

– I am here. I . . . I . . .

The voice came back to him where he stood near the tree. His shadow was on the ground. It was the shadow of a tall man like his father. It swayed with the movement of the trees and the voice vibrated between the walls of the palace and made the shutters shake. Eyes closed in sleep opened, let out a pale gleam and closed again.

– I am here . . . I . . . I . . .

The echo came back to him again like a faint whistle. His ears strained themselves to hear. The voice sounded familiar. It resembled the voice of his father and was hoarse with a slight cracked note in its tones where he pronounced *I*... His lips pressed themselves together with disdain after the final *y* sound in the *I*.

   – I . . . I . . . I . . .

His father was sitting in his high-backed chair dressed in his military uniform. Over his chest lay round discs that shone with a red glare. His shoulders were broad, padded with cotton, and his nose stuck out prominently. It had a big, cartilaginous hook. He held out his neck like a turkey-cock and his voice resounded throughout the house.

   – I . . . I . . . I . . . I . . .

It went through the window of the hall and crossed over to their neighbours. So his mother bolted the shutters and closed the glass windows, then stood with her back to the wall and her face towards him. Her face was drained of all its blood, white as a sheet, and it looked even whiter against the black muslin dress she was wearing. Her legs were white. She held them pressed close together, and the blue veins showed under the skin. Her lips moved but no sound came out of them as though she were talking to herself or to some phantom which only his father could see.

His eyes circled with his head around the room as he sat in his high-backed chair. The small eyes were searching from behind his eyeglasses for this phantom. They went round and round the room looking behind the clothes-stand, inside the cupboard and then under the bed.

He could not understand how the body of his father which seemed to him so huge could bend down with all its hugeness and look under the bed. But it did. He could see him as he got down on his knees as though praying, with his neck stretched out to get his head under the bed. He was still a baby. He had not learnt to speak, but his eyes could see, and his ears could pick up sounds and voices. And at night when he lay in bed he could hear his father's voice coming from under the bed.

– Where are you, Eblis?

The name rang in his ears as he lay curled up around himself like an embryo. He closed his eyes and hid himself under the eiderdown. In his dreams he could see the Devil standing in the dark. He was wearing his mother's black muslin dress and his face was also black, but his teeth were white. They flashed in the night as though he were smiling scornfully at something, or baring his fangs. In the morning his eyes opened to light filtering in through the shutters in faint lines. When his mother gave him a glass of milk, he emptied it into the wash-basin.

– Drink your milk!

– I won't!

– Do what you're told, boy.

– I won't!

He did not obey his mother. He had heard his father saying that women were lacking in mind and in their faith in God. At school he had heard his teacher say that men were custodians. The teacher made him open the book and read out the phrase: *Men are the custodians of women*, and every day he was made to read it out and repeat it three times after the teacher. The teacher pursed his lips as he pronounced the second syllable of the word *custodians* making it as long as he could for emphasis. The boys would chant after him in unison:

– *Custodians*.

He put up his hand and asked:

– Sir, what does the word *custodian* mean?

The teacher wore a red fez which hung down over his ears and carried a black fly-whisk like a horse's tail with which he chased away the flies.

– To be a custodian means to be sovereign over someone.

– And what does *to be sovereign* mean, sir?

– Sovereign means that the male rules over the female, boy, and that the female submits to the male.

The word *male* kept ringing out in his teacher's voice. The teacher's voice resembled his father's voice. He too had a high-backed chair. His neck stretched upwards and his lips pronounced the word male with a prolonged resonance which made him sound like a he-goat.

– Maaaaaale.

He did not know what the word *male* meant. He asked his mother, and when he asked her she hit him over the hand. Her hand was big and his was much smaller, so he hid it away from her in the pocket of his school uniform. It was made of white cotton with red squares and had a circular collar raised around the neck like his sister's uniform. His sister walked to school with him. She trod down on the ground just as he did and wore the same black leather shoes, but without laces.

When he put on his shoes he pulled the laces and knotted them exactly in the same way as his father, and when he knotted his tie he stretched his neck upwards imitating what he had seen him do. It appeared to him that a male was distinguished by the things he tied in his shoe and around his neck. But the boys in school made fun of him when he said that. They led him to the water-closet and it was behind its closed door that he discovered the truth.

When he first saw the truth it looked meaningless to him. It was just a piece of flesh hanging down below his belly, and from which the stream of his urine flowed out. Yet the eyes of the boys in school gleamed with pride when they looked at it. They measured the piece of flesh with a ruler and each one of them shouted at once:

– I am bigger . . . I . . . I . . .

The voice of the Headman's son rose louder than the voice of any other boy. He opened his mouth as wide as he could, and shouted. His chest rose and fell. The beating under his ribs grew stronger. Drums beat to the same rhythm, and the boys shouted in unison. They carried him on their shoulders. Their voices resounded in his ears like the roar of a waterfall. They seemed to fuse into a single sound. I am bigger . . . I . . . I.

He stood still for a moment, lifting his eyes, looking towards the window. Behind the fine curtain was a light like the flame of an oil-lamp wick which trembled. Her silhouette came and went behind the glass. Her breasts were big like his mother's and a chain hung down between them. At the end of the chain was a disc. It was shining like gold in the sun.

He swallowed his tears and buried his head in her chest as though she were his mother. Since the day his father had slapped his face, he had never wept again.

– You boy, there, I don't want to see you weeping like a woman again.

He clenched his teeth and hid his pain. The tears gathered under his ribs to form something like a swelling. At night his mother tiptoed to his side and covered him. When he woke up in the morning he pouted his lips at her. He had seen his father doing that when he sat in the high-backed chair.

– I . . . I . . . I am greater, greater [1] . . .

He stood up on the chair. That way he became taller than his mother. She put a quill between his fingers and told him to draw a tree and birds. He did not like drawing. He trod on leaves with his shoes, aimed stones at birds with a sling, and stuck the quill into his hair like a feather. He put on a military coat and waved a sword in front of his mother's face.

– Where is Eblis?

The name Eblis resounded in the air like a shot from a gun. It echoed through the dark spaces around the palace. The trees bent their heads to the wind. The sound passed between the crumbling walls, and down the corridors and reached the male ward, plunged in darkness.

Eblis was lying on his back. He opened his eyes. He glimpsed him standing in the opening of the door wearing his father's long white robe and the turban of Sheikh Masoud around his head, with the feather sticking out from the top as though he were the Headman of the Village.

– Get up Eblis. Get up now, immediately.

He pronounced the words *get up* the way his father used to do. They escaped from his mouth through clenched teeth.

He closed his eyes and hid himself under the eiderdown. But the big hand with its large bony fingers

[1] In Arabic the same word is used for bigger and for greater.

crept towards him and jerked the eiderdown off his body.

– Get up, boy, and go about your business.

– I beg of you. Leave me to sleep.

– Sleep? How can you be left to sleep, Eblis?

– Like all the other creatures of God.

– And who will go around whispering temptations into people's ears?

His voice echoed loudly in his ears like the voice of God. But his fingers were stained yellow, and his breath smelt of tobacco. There was the odour of sweat under his armpits like Sheikh Masoud.

He pushed his hand quickly under the pillow and felt for the half-cigarette which he had hidden under it.

– Give me that cigarette, boy!

– No.

– No! What do you mean, *No*?

– It means no.

– Don't you know who I am, boy?

– I know . . . I know, Chief.

– Chief, you ass! I am above everyone. Right above.

But there was no one higher than the General. That was what he had heard from his fellow soldiers. The General walked in front with his soldiers behind him. His body was fleshy and white. He wore a leather jacket like the bears in the land of the eskimos. He appeared on television on the CNN. When he walked he had a slight limp, and he advanced with a slow step. He lifted his right leg in front of him without bending his knee, as though it were made of wood. His cheeks filled up with air, and the blood rushed to his face from the upward movement of his leg. His lips were red, and the lower lip hung down over his chin. It trembled when the guns fired their missiles with a loud sound. He lifted his eyes up and scanned the skies, watched the dark phantoms hovering in the clouds like birds of prey. They had steel wings and from their bellies dropped bombs like big drops of black rain. Dust and particles of sand rose up in the air, and the world became enveloped in a yellow fog. The air was heavy with smoke and the smell of burning oil.

The General clapped his hands with glee. He threw his head back and peals of laughter rang out from between his lips. He lifted his hand with the V sign and shouted at the top of his voice:

– Victory!

The drums rolled, and the soldiers stood in a line on either side of the street, their faces to the walls and their backs to the people. Behind the General walked the High Sheikh dressed in king's clothes. Over his shoulders he wore a cape embroidered in gold thread and his head was enveloped in a white veil. Near the High Sheikh was the Director and near the Director was the Head Nurse wearing her white tunic. The whistle moved up and down over her breasts. Bringing up the rear was a band and Zanouba the dancer swaying her hips, clacking brass castanets as she danced.

– Your love burns like a fire, my sweet, my beloved country.

The General stopped suddenly. His eyes opened wide in amazement, and he stammered:

– Oh, no. No . . . It's . . . It's unbelievable.

The word *unbelievable* pierced his ears. He scratched his head and looked around with questioning eyes. No one could understand the language spoken by the General except the Director, and the Chief of the Army. The Head Nurse could follow a few words like 'thank you'. The General used to pronounce it in a special way. The tip of his tongue protruded with the *th* and he bowed down with his hat in his hands.

– Thank you, Missis President.

But he did not know any foreign words at all. The only word he knew was *no*. He was familiar with it from the day he was born. The cat squatted next to him and mewed: No! No! His sister played hopscotch with him, jumped on one leg and laughed all the time repeating: No! No! She opened her copy book and with her pen wrote an *n* and then an *o*. But Sheikh Masoud pulled the pen out of her hands and beat her with his stick on her buttocks.

– Away with you, Nefissa, there's no place for you here. Go back to your mother.

– Please, Sheikh Masoud, for the Prophet's sake. I want to learn to write.

– Write? Write what, you girl? You little nothing.

At night he slept near her on the mat. He could hear her quietly sobbing. He imagined himself hiding the copy book and the pencil under her pillow. When Sheikh Masoud beat her with his cane stick, he aimed a stone at the Sheikh's turban with his sling, and caught it in his hands before it fell to the ground.

– Come here, you boy, Eblis.

The Sheikh would run after him with his stick, but his mother came to his rescue. She snatched the stick away from him, and waved her big hard hand at him.

– Why do you beat him, Sheikh Masoud?

– He's an impudent rascal. Nobody has taught him any manners.

– He's been brought up better than anyone else.

– Brought up by women?

Sheikh Masoud pouted his lips after he pronounced the word *women* as though expelling spit from his mouth. Then he turned his back on her. The back of his neck was thick and fleshy, and he held it up like a turkey-cock. He walked with a slow step, holding the cane in his hand. On top of his head the turban moved steadily through the air. The Village Headman would be walking on the bank of the river surrounded by the village guards. As soon as Sheikh Masoud spotted him, his big fleshy neck would shrink to the size of a sesame seed. He advanced towards the Headman with bent head, bowed down over his hand and kissed it.

Eblis's mother would be standing nearby, her head held straight up in the air. Eblis stood beside her holding her hand. Sheikh Masoud nudged him in the shoulder with the point of his stick.

– Boy, salute our Headman, and kiss his hand.

She pulled her son by the hand and walked off with him, her face looking towards the sun, and her back to the Village Headman. Her head was always like that, held high up. It never bent towards the ground. And her eyes were always wide open, facing straight ahead. She whispered:

– Never kiss anybody's hand. We live by the sweat of our brow. Never kiss any one's hand.

Her voice floated over his closed eyelids like a song that went on as long as the longest night. He lay on the mat and his sister thrust her hand under the pillow. She opened the copy book and wrote down her name: Nefissa. It had seven letters. She laughed loudly and repeated:

– Nefissa, Nefissa! You'll fly out of the cage.

She jumped on one leg as they played hopscotch. A bird on the branch of the tree looked down on her and repeated: Chirp, Chirp. The cat waved its tail and mewed: Meow, meow. The children sang:

– Whistle o train, I'm going home.

Then they held one another's tails and whistled:

Toot, toot. The goat leapt into the air and said: Maa, Maa. The cow stopped turning the water-wheel and made a joyful sound: Moo, moo, moo! The donkey lifted its head to the sky, opened its jaws wide and brayed with a noise which sounded like prolonged laughter: Hee-haw, hee-haw, hee-haw. The snake peered out from a crack, moved its tail from one side to the other, and its eyes shone with a mischievous gleam.

Suddenly the laughter ceased. All sound died away and the world was plunged in darkness. He closed his eyes and hid his head under the covers. He could hear a voice call out.

– Where are you, Eblis?

A cane nudged him in the shoulder.

– Stand up, boy, and salute.

It was the General's voice. But he was speaking in Arabic. Eblis half-opened one eye and peered out. He could see him standing in front of him, just as he used to see him when he was a child, leaning on the door, wearing his dead man's white robe, and the turban of Sheikh Masoud.

– Speak up, Eblis.

– What shall I say, o God?

– Confess.

– Confess to what?

– Did you whisper anything in the General's ear?

– Me?

– Yes, you. Who else?

– How could I whisper in the General's ear?

– The way you whisper in everybody's ears.
The General does not know Arabic. How can I whisper
things in his ear?

He hid his head under the eiderdown. In his ears
echoed the sound of a child breathing deeply. The
breathing was interrupted, gasping, like sobs. The cane
whistled through the air. There was a hoarse guttural
voice speaking nearby. It was the voice of the Head of
the village guard. The butt of his rifle hit the ground.

– National service, boy!

He hid in the storage yard, curled around himself
like an embryo, deep between the bundles of cotton
sticks. He held his breath and the beating under his
ribs seemed to stop. He could hear nothing except the
occasional howl of a wolf, or bark of a dog. Then
silence reigned and the moon came out from behind
the clouds. The white light stole through the dry stalks
of maize. A long arm reached out. It had five fingers.
It caught hold of him like it would a hen. He felt his
robe being lifted over his back, and his underpants,
made of rough dark cotton, pulled down. The moonlight fell on his trembling buttocks. His back was to
the light and his front faced the other way. He was
afraid to turn round and look. He was afraid to move
his head to where the other stood, to lift his eyes up
to him. He was big, much bigger than him. His body

shed a long shadow on the ground, and he was still a child. He had not learnt to read yet. He sat on the mat next to the other boys, held his legs pressed close together under the rough cotton robe, with his arms folded around his chest.

The stick nudged him in the ribs.

– Recite the verse, boy.

He closed his eyes and breathed deeply.

– *And Lot said unto his people . . .*

He swallowed his saliva with a sucking noise.

– *In lust for men you fornicate with them instead of women, for you are a corrupt people.*

The stick nudged him again in the shoulder.

– Not that verse, you ass! The verse of Eblis.

He closed his eyes and opened his mouth.

– *And God said unto his angels: I shall appoint a viceroy on the earth to rule in my name. They said: And why shouldst thou appoint him who will spread evil and shed blood?*

He swallowed his saliva.

– *And they all bowed down and worshipped the corrupt viceroy, all except Eblis.*

Sheikh Bassiouni stared at him with bloodshot eyes.

– The viceroy was not corrupt, you ass.

– Then who sowed corruption and shed blood on the earth?

– You dare to answer back, boy?

– I . . . ?

– Not another word!

His voice broke off suddenly. He looked round at the boys. Their eyes met under a cloud. On every eye lay a white spot and black flies. The stick rained its blows down on their backs. The stick of the Sheikh at school, then that of the Head of the village guards. The razor-blade ran over their heads, shaving off the hair. They were crowded into the armoured truck, and their shaven heads looked out between the iron bars. Their faces were long and thin like those of old people. Their eyes were wide open, full of wonder like children. Behind them was another armoured truck carrying sheep. Their shaven heads looked out at the road leading to the slaughter house.

Pouring out from radio sets was the voice of Zanouba singing a song:

– Tonight is the feast; joy to the world.

In the pale light he could see Zanouba's face. Her features were familiar. He had seen them before. Her skin had a dark pallor, she opened her mouth as wide as she could and closed her eyes. She stamped her feet on the ground, and waved her arms wildly in the air. Her breast rose and fell as she gasped out:

– Tonight is the feast! Tonight is the feast.

The soldiers stamped their heels on the ground. They lifted their guns to their shoulders with closed eyes. They slept standing up. They woke up from their sleep shouting out:

– Tonight is the feast! The feast! Long live! Long live!

He slipped out from under the eiderdown and ran on his barefeet. He ran through the unending spaces of darkness. The brass helmet fell off his head. His uniform dropped down over his buttocks to his feet. His back was uncovered, exposed to the fortunes of the wind. The Khamaseen winds lashed him from behind. He swallowed dust and coarse particles of sand. The whip rose in the air, then came down on him. He could hear it hiss down through the air, but he felt no pain. And when he went into the water-closet he could see the marks on his back. They were long and they twisted like the tails of serpents and were as red as blood.

– Say *I'm a mara.*[1]

The mouth opened wide and spat full in his face.

– You son of a *mara.*

– My mother was worth twenty men.

He lifted his head in the same way as his mother did and stiffened the muscles of his back. The Director stared at him with wide-open eyes, then brought his mouth close up to the General's ear and whispered.

– Inherited madness, sir!

The General nodded his head, filled his cheeks with air and said:

[1] *Mara* means a woman in popular language and is used here as an insult. To call a man a woman in the Arab culture, as in most cultures, is insulting.

147

– Yes! Yes! Yes!

He was chewing something. The cat by his side mewed and rubbed itself against his legs. It pulled his underpants down. The Director hit out at the cat with his stick.

– Stop! Go away! Stop! Stop!

The soldiers hid their laughter, covering their mouths with their hands like boys in a class. They closed their eyes and yawned. The Sheikh walked down the rows, beating them on their buttocks with his cane. All except the son of the Headman. He threw his head back and laughed in a loud voice.

– I am above everyone else.

His voice echoed in the air, and the echo went on.

– I am above everyone else.

The cat leapt forwards and stuck out its claws. It mewed in a shrill voice, and its long tail curled like that of a serpent.

– Meow! Meow! Meow!

The soldiers, dressed in white robes, lifted the guns to their shoulders and shouted out in one voice:

– Meow! Meow! Meow!

The police sirens shrieked, bullets could be heard exploding in the air. He hid his head under the eider-down. He heard a voice say:

– Come out from there, Eblis.

– I swear by God I'm innocent, it's not me!

– Then who is it, boy?

– It's the serpent, sir!

– Oh no. It's impossible. It's unbelievable.

– Yes, believe me sir. The serpent is the source of all trouble.

– How come, boy?

– If it weren't for the serpent we would all have been in Paradise long ago.

– Oh no! Arrest him!

– I swear by God I'm innocent, sir.

The Head Nurse came out. Behind her were male nurses carrying ropes. He hid his head under the eider-down, and fell asleep. In his ears he could hear a prolonged whistle like a buzz, or like the sound of quiet sobbing that went on through the night.

– Nou, nou, nou, nou, nou!

10 *Sinful Love*

She could hear the voice floating in the air over her closed eyelids. It resembled the voice of her dead son when he stood near her bed in the darkness. The hair on his head was black and thick. His eyes, too, were black and in them shimmered a tear that neither dried nor dropped out. His nose was straight, unlike that of his father.

She held out her hand and took hold of his. His fingers were long like hers, and the tips were fine. He played music with them, and the light of dawn broke through, and birds chirped up on the trees. She opened her mouth to sing with him but her voice made no sound. A leather belt was tied round her chest, and her lids were closed.

She strained her ears. Was that her name being called out? It was as though she had never heard it before. She opened her eyes. She could see the grubby, cracked ceiling. The plaster had fallen off in places leaving a design which looked like the god Ra'a but with the head of the Ibis calf. His eyes were bulging. It was as though she had never seen them before, yet she felt she had been seeing them every day, day after day, and year after year, for thirty years. For thirty years now he had not ceased looking at her with those two eyes of his, inside walls of brick and cement, and a high fence which rose around them on every side and hid the horizon, and her at the window, waiting. The sky was a black pit during the night, a grey pit during the day, and the pit surrounded her, separated her from people. Another pit separated her body from her self. A big garden surrounded the palace. There were pallid flowers, like the flowers laid on tombstones; and there were long corridors dark at night, silent during the day, except for the sound of wheels on the asphalt road, or the noise of a distant horn. She stood at the window waiting for tomorrow.

Her father called tomorrow *the unknown*; her mother called it the future. She could see it open up in front of her like the horizon, and when the sun rose she ran through green spaces, the pleats of her orange-coloured dress billowing with air, and carrying her along on wings. Around her neck she wore a wide white collar, and in her hand she carried her school satchel with its copy books and pens inside.

At the corner of the street she stopped to look round. She could see her mother's face at the window, shining like a star in the distance. She lifted her hand and waved to her. At the door of the school she met her friend. They played hopscotch together in the yard, and in the reading lesson they recited the poem. Its verses ran through her head like music. At night she held her pen and wrote a love letter to God.

– You are love. You are the morning star. The light of my heart.

She moved the tip of the pen over the surface of the paper. Her grandmother watched her as she lay by her side.

– What are you writing, Ganat?

– A letter to God.

Her grandmother made the sign of the cross.

– *Our Father which art in Heaven forgive us our tres-passes.*

She moistened her greying lips with water, then put the glass on top of the small cupboard. She called it the *commodino*.[1] She recited a verse from the Bible under her breath, closed the book and put it under her pillow, then shut her eyes and muttered something. After a little while she opened her eyes again and stared at her silently.

– Why are you still awake, Ganat?

– Sleep does not want to come to me.

– Go to sleep, Ganat.

– Would you like to hear a poem?

---

[1] Taken from the French or Italian. A small commode placed beside the bed.

– A poem?

Her grandmother let out a long sigh. She stretched out her veined neck and took a deep breath, then expelled it with a noise that sounded like a prolonged whistle. She sucked at her lips. Her lower lip dropped down over her flabby chin, lying in a fold over her neck.

A poem?!

She closed her eyes and muttered.

– *Our Father which art in Heaven.*

She opened her eyes and their look met.

– Go to sleep, Ganat. Chase the eye of the Devil away.

– The Devil?

– Your grandfather used to call it *the Devil of poetry.*[1]

Her grandmother's lips opened in a smile, then contracted and twisted her mouth to one side. She leaned on her elbow and got out of bed, slipping her feet into the slippers. She called her slippers *pantoufli.*[2] She moved away from the bed with her slow, crawling step, and put a square cushion on the floor, then squatted down on it breathing hard. She stretched her hand under the bed and pulled out a long wooden box that resembled a coffin.

She watched her from the bed. She saw her make

---

[1] Like the muse. Art is often associated with the Devil in the Arab culture.
[2] *Pantoufle* in French.

the sign of the cross over her breast, then open the box with a wrinkled hand that trembled. A smell of naphthalene, [1] or formalin as her grandmother called it, rose in the air. She hid her head under the covers thinking that her grandfather's body lay stretched out in the box. Instead she saw a white dress with flounces and lace as delicate as butterflies' wings. The bridal veil was made of fine chiffon. The dress had a long train which trailed over the ground and her grandmother folded it up, one layer over the other. In her eyes she could see a film of water like tears that neither fell nor dried up. At the bottom of the box lay an exercise book with a pale yellow cover. Its edges were worn. She lifted it out and brought it close up under her eyes until it almost touched her nose. She closed her lids and slept as she sat, opened them again and started to arrange the balls of naphthalene in rows inside the box, then put the Bible back where it had lain.

At night, Ganat could hear her laugh with a sound that resembled weeping. She repeated words in a chanting voice as though she were singing.

– Naphthalene eats up the moths, and moths eat up the Bible, and fire eats up the moths, and who will go to Paradise? I shall go! I shall enter Paradise! I! I!

Her voice choked as she counted each *I* on her fingers: I! I! Its tones began to break like her grandfather's voice in the morning when he repeated:

[1] Mothballs.

– I am going to Paradise, and you are going to Hell.
I am going to Paradise! I! I! I! Paradise . . . Paradise,
and you: Hell! Hell! Where's the tea? This tea is cold.
I want hot tea! Very hot tea like fire,[1] like fire!

He coughed and spat into the wash-basin, knocked
the floor with his stick, sipped tea from his glass with
a loud noise, coughed out phlegm into his white hand-
kerchief, and then threw it into the clothes-basket.

At the bottom of the clothes-basket lay his underpants made of fine linen. They resembled women's
underwear and had no legs. Her grandmother called
them *cut* and she held them between her fingers,
brought them close up to her nose, smelt them and
then pouted her lips.

– He went to her yesterday.

– To whom, Nena?

– A woman who's eating up his mind.

– Like the moths, Nena?

– Yes, exactly!

– Is Grandfather going to Heaven or to Hell?

– Your grandfather will be thrown headlong into
Hell.

She closed her eyes and slept. In her dreams she
saw her grandfather roasting on a fire. He was turning
on a spit over the flames. His head looked like that of
a sheep being roasted for the feast. Before dawn, her
body would begin to shake in the bed. She could hear

[1] *El Nar* in Arabic means both fire and Hell.

the posts knocking and she could see her grandmother get up from her bed and go over to the clothes-basket. She took out her grandfather's underpants, holding them between her thumb and her index finger like a dead cockroach, then she threw them into a basin, poured kerosene over them and lit them with a match. The flames rose up in the bathroom, long and red and writhing like the tails of serpents. She heard her grandmother's scream coming through the closed door, as long as the longest of dark nights.

– Yahou ou ou ou ou ou!

It was as though her grandmother were calling on Jehovah. She had read about him in the Holy Bible. He was the God of volcanoes and earthquakes. Her grandmother beseeched him to flood the earth and shake it with earthquakes so that the Day of Judgement would be near, and everyone would get what he deserved.

She could feel the bed shaking under her. Its brass posts made a rattling noise. Her mother said it was the spirit of her grandmother that had come back to revenge itself on her grandfather. She hid her head under the eiderdown and stretched out her arms over the bed as far as they would go. Her hand hit the wall. There was no one in the bed beside her. She opened her eyes. A faint light filtered through the slats of the shutters. The light blue curtain waved to and fro in the air. The ceiling was painted with a coat of white plastic paint and the bed no longer had brass posts. It was a wide bed, and had been carried into the house with the rest of the bride's furniture.

On the wall hung a picture which resembled the picture of her mother on her wedding night. But the young woman in the picture was not smiling. She was wearing a white wedding gown which looked like a funeral shroud, and she carried a bouquet of pale flowers on her arm. They looked like the flowers of a funeral wreath. Standing by her side was a tall man whose broad shoulders were padded with cotton. He was dressed in a military uniform. On his chest was a medal, and his nose was a big hook of cartilage under tight skin.

– Zakaria?

The name sounded strange to her ears as though she had never heard it before, or as though it had echoed in her ears every day, day after day, and year after year for thirty years, as she stood in the dark waiting for him. Her head dropped forwards over her chest as she stood preparing his dinner. She waited for him hour after hour, but he did not come. If he came he was in a hurry to eat. After he had eaten he was in a hurry to sleep without making love or after making love as fast as he could, like swallowing food without chewing it.

He took off his military uniform and the medal, felt his name engraved on the golden disc with the tips of his fingers and caressed it as one would caress the soft head of a child. Then he put it in the box lined with green velvet. He took off his trousers and his vest. He hid his underwear in the clothes-basket, looking at her out of the corner of his eye. She closed her eyelids and fell asleep. Before the light of dawn broke through she got out of bed. She could see his underpants curled up around their guilt at the bottom of the basket.

In the morning she would see him in the picture standing in the front row. His eyes were bulging and his hands were clasped over his belly. He held his legs close together like a virgin, walked up to shake hands with the General, bowed down and then stepped backwards, colliding with the belly of the man standing behind him, stepping on his toes with the heel of his boot.

The General called out to him suddenly. He rushed forwards, forgetting that between him and the General was a glass door. His nose hit against the door, and its hooked cartilage gave way, his eyeglasses falling on the floor and breaking into small pieces. He retreated backwards quickly and his buttocks collided with another glass door. He kept moving round and round in a glass box that let in light but no air. His eyes bulged more and more. His broad chest rose and fell as though he were choking under the iron armour.

In the picture she could see his pale face looking out from behind the glass. He did a complete turn in the revolving door to find himself face to face with the General.

– Good morning, Your Excellency General. Everything's in order, sir! Everything's okay.

But the General was as silent as a white bear. His cheeks filled up with air. His red lips opened to let out a noise like a hiss.

– Oh! No! The Devil.

Eblis in the language of the General was the Devil. He stuck out his tongue when he pronounced *the*.

– Yes, *za*[1] Devil, sir.

He turned *the* into *za* but the General's interpreter tried to show him how to pronounce it correctly by putting his tongue out between his teeth, and asked him to make a statement in which he made clear that the Devil was the source of all evil in the world. He was the only one who had refused to listen to reason, and had insisted on saying no, whereas all the others without exception had knelt in worship, and not dared to lift up their eyes.

– The Devil!

The General opened the Bible. His fleshy white fingers covered with carroty hairs turned over the pages. He made the sign of the cross over his broad chest covered with a steel armoured plate. Then he issued the order in an incisive, cutting voice:

[1] Egyptians often have difficulty in pronouncing *the* and tend to say *za*.

– Kill the Devil.

The soldiers repeated in unison as they aimed their fire:

– Kill the Devil.

They did not put their tongues out between their teeth as they should have done. Their tongues stuck to their palates, and their throats were dry. Over their eyes was a moist film like tears. Their faces were thin and pale, their eyelids eaten away by the flies which settled on them as they sat on the river bank. The bones of their shoulder-blades protruded. Under the military uniforms were long red lines that twisted like the tails of serpents. The sound of whips whistled through the air. Their breathing came in rapid gasps. Thousands of voices panted out in unison:

– Down! Down!

The sound of their voices roared in her ears like a waterfall, as she ran in the dark, carried by the four wheels. Her mouth was open and she panted:

– Down! Down!

The sound shook the bed under her and the brass made a clicking noise. The many voices fused into a single long whistle. She exerted an effort to open her eyes but she was deep in sleep. She stretched out her arm as far as the wall. His place near the wall was empty. He was there a moment ago. He had been there for thirty years, and he could have stayed on there for just another moment. But she did not hold him back.

She let him go out of her life. She did not open her eyes to keep him back. She did not open her mouth to call him. For thirty years she had said: Zakaria. He could have waited for her to open her mouth and shout:

– Down with the system.

She heard her voice echo in her ears so she opened up a narrow slit between her lids. She was afraid to open them wide lest the dream become reality. Above her head was the grubby ceiling. The plaster had fallen off in parts leaving a design like that of the god Ra'a with the body of a human being and the head of a calf. An electric lamp hung from a wire to which were stuck the bodies of dead flies. The door of the room opened. A faint light stole in from the corridor. She saw him come in with his tall figure and his head held upright. The hair on his head was thick and black. A single lock fell over his forehead. He lifted it up with a long finger. His eyes met her eyes.

– Ganat?

He put his arms around her as though she were his dead mother. Her skin was dark and unwrinkled. It shone under the sun like burnished copper. Her hair was long and black. It flew around her with the wind. She threw it back with a single movement of the head, like a mare owned by no one, free.

She rose from her bed with a gliding movement, ran on her bare feet to the kitchen and returned with a bottle of chilled beer, fresh cucumber sliced into long fingers which she put in a glass, and a plate of white cheese cut into small cubes. She put the knife on the table close to the vase of flowers. A single flower hung from it, its leaves shrivelled up and its petals pale white without a single hint of life-blood in them.

She tiptoed back to the kitchen and came back with a jug of water. She moistened the flower with one drop of water after another. The transparent curtain trembled over the window in a soft breeze that blew with the rise of dawn. The morning star shone in the sky like the eyes of her mother looking at her from a distance as she walked to school. She turned round and waved to her. A gleam rose to the surface of her eyes like tears that remained unshed by the sky, and neither dried nor dropped down. The vase was filled up with water and the dying petals moved in the breeze. The flower opened up under the light of dawn, and the red sunrise crept across the pale white sky.

– Ganat?

He heard her laugh. Her laugh rang out in the silent night like silver. She threw her hair back and laughed. Her laugh hovered over her head like circles of light. Suddenly she was silent. A cloud crept over her eyes. At the height of her happiness, the sadness in her depths rose to the surface.

She tore her eyes away from the horizon and looked at him. His eyes were full of light. She wound her arms

around him as though he were her dead son. He wore
a shirt made of white cotton open at the neck. Under
his armpit he had black hair. It smelt like children. On
his back under his shoulder-blade was an old wound.

– I love you.

The word *love* echoed strangely in her ears, as
though she were hearing it for the first time. He sat
opposite her on the northern balcony, drinking from
the glass without making a sound. He chewed his food
without making a sound, too. His features were familiar. It was as though she had been used to seeing them
since the day she was born. When he saw her his eyes
would fill up with a light like that in her mother's eyes.
His voice stole over her eyelids like a warm ray.

– I love you.

Her eyes opened wide in wonder. She felt the beat
under her ribs change into a dance. The ears of corn
in the fields waved to the same rhythm, and the butterflies fluttered their wings to an old melody. Her
ears were now hearing their sounds. Thousands of
wings fluttering, thousands of hands raised in the air
waving and the sound of voices like a waterfall singing.

– I love you! I love you!

The ground under her trembled, and the bed standing on its legs over the ground trembled too. The four
walls swayed with a visible movement. The picture on
the wall trembled and fell to the ground, its glass breaking into small pieces which flew into the air like drops

of rain. The wedding veil flew in the air and the flounces of her dress rose on wings. The lace hovered around her in the air like wisps of cotton. A white spray collected around the clouds.

She saw him rise out of the picture and emerge from amidst the rain and the broken glass, wearing his military uniform with the medal on his breast. He was wearing her grandfather's dead face. His head was square like that of a white bear, held steadily up in the air like that of Aboul Houl. It had a sharp edge at the top like the Pyramid of Khoufou. His nose was a cartilaginous hook resembling the beak of an eagle.

She saw him walk towards her in the dark. The night was black without stars or moon, except for one star that shone faintly through a thin wisp of cloud. The air was heavy with dust and particles of sand. The heads of trees shed their dark shadows on the ground, like phantoms. His eyes were looking around amidst the shadows. He searched behind the clothes-stand, inside the cupboard, and on top of the shelf near the ceiling. He knelt down the way her grandfather used to do, and looked under the bed, his face to the floor and his buttocks up in the air, as though he were praying.

– Where's Eblis?

She was standing at the window like her mother used to do. Her eyes would be lifted to the sky, fastened on the only star hanging above the horizon. She sang to it in a low voice, weeping quietly:

– O Zahra, mother of the Universe. You who know the secrets of the world.

His face behind her was reflected in the glass of the window. His skin was grey like the stones of the Mokattam Hills. His hair had fallen from his head. A few strands remained above his ears and they waved like feathers in the air. His eyes were fastened on the knife, near the vase. Two glasses stood on the marble-topped table. The earth trembled and with it the table which stood on it. The two glasses touched with a singing crystal sound.

Her ears strained themselves to hear as she stood with her back to him, and her face to the window. The beating under her ribs grew stronger. One glass touched the other making the same sound again, echoing like an old melody, and she was running through the green spaces, racing after the butterflies.

In the glass of the window she saw his hand reach out over the table. The sharp blade of the knife shone in the moonlight like a long flash of lightning. It lit up her face like a flare and her face was the face of death, enveloped in a white dress.

She turned round quickly before his hand could strike. The knife cut through her flesh making a wound in her back below the shoulder. Had she not turned round to face him at that moment the knife could have gone through to her heart.

The lights fell on his face where he stood surrounded

by his soldiers, his henchmen, his attendants and his slaves. No one could raise his eyes up to him without being struck blind by his light, without falling to the ground shivering with fright.

She lifted her head and looked him in the face with wide-open eyes. She looked steadily at the knife. Her face in the glass was the face of her dead grandmother, and blood flowed from her in a long, thin stream like it had flowed from her mother's body. He stood in front of her, his tall stature and his broad shoulders enveloped in the body of her dead father.

– Dishonour can only be washed away by blood.

He advanced towards her with the knife. She did not step back. She stood there looking at him with wide-open eyes. Her eyes were big and shining and his face was reflected in them. He saw nothing but his own face when he looked into her eyes. He stood stock still for a moment, examining his features. It was as though he were seeing his face for the first time. His nose was broken, flattened like the nose of the Sphinx. His eyes were small and beady. They were yellow in colour like the eyes of a snake, and his skin was dark, like the face of the Devil.

He shivered as though suddenly coming to his senses. He realised he was seeing the face of the other man she saw in her eyes.

She was a fallen woman, a whore like her mother and her grandmother. All women were whores. They had no brains, they lacked faith in God. His father had said so. They were the accomplices of the Devil. They opened the doors to Hell. That was what his grandfather had always told him. They were the source of all evil, the cause of sin as was written in the Bible. Their vengeance was terrible. He had learnt that in the Koran.

He stood in front of her like a statue. His fingers were tight around the knife, his eyes wide open, staring into space. The whites of his eyes were bulging. They had a yellowish tinge shot with fine strands of blood. His pupils seemed to turn round on themselves like small, black beads.

As they turned he missed her. She stood still, her eye on the knife he was holding. She reached her hand out for it with a quick movement. The blade shone like a ray of lightning, and suddenly the knife was in her hand.

He stepped backwards quickly. Her hand was smaller than his, her bones lighter than his bones, but the stronger of the two was the one who was armed.

– Fallen man. Whore of a man.

His lips opened to answer but no sound came from them. Like his father and his grandfather he had wanted to say that a man was not dishonoured if he went to another woman. But a woman was low, was a whore by nature, even if she wore a veil, and was clothed in virtue. He had thought she was different from other women, that he would be the only man in her life, the one and only God. And now he was losing her for ever. Now at this very moment he was losing her for ever. He had never loved her as much as he did now at this moment when he was losing her. He felt like kissing her hand, asking for forgiveness. His breath moved with a panting sound, in and out of his chest. His chest rose and fell, shaking the golden medal so that it shimmered under the lights. His name was engraved deeply on it in letters written with curved and jagged lines: *El Sayed Zakaria El Abd.*[1]

– *El Sayed* Zakaria *El Abd?*

When she looked at the letters of his name they were stretched out in front of her like the legs of a beetle. It was as though she were seeing his name for the first time. Master and slave together in one name. Her dead grandfather's voice echoed in her ear.

– I am your master and the slave of the *Mamour.*[2]

She hid her head under the covers. Her grandmother lay next to her breathing deeply. The brass posts of the bed were shaking. Around her head she had wound a black scarf. The Bible was under her pillow. Her eyes were closed and her lips were moving as she murmured under her breath:

– *Thou shalt crawl on thy belly forever and man shall rule over thee.*

[1] *El Sayed* means the master and *El Abd* the slave: Master Zakaria the slave.
[2] *Mamour* means he who receives orders from others.

She looked out with one eye from under the eider-down. Her gaze met the wide open eyes of her grand-mother.

– Who is the *Mamour*, Nena?

– He's your father's chief at work.

– Why is he called *Mamour*, then?

– Because he has a boss above him who gives him orders.

– Who is above him, Nena?

– The Governor of the Province.

– And who's above the Governor, Nena?

– The King.

– And who's above the King, Nena?

– The *Khawaga*[1] General.

– And who's above the General, Nena?

– Our God.

Her grandmother drew the sign of the cross over her breast.

– *Our father which art in Heaven forgive us our tres-passes.*

From behind the glass window she could see the flames like red tongues reaching to the ceiling. Her grandmother lay on the tiled floor of the bathroom, her lips tightly closed. The silence echoed in her ears like the roar of a waterfall. Thousands of voices were shouting:

[1] *Khawaga* is a term used to indicate a foreigner. It implies contradictory feelings, fear of the coloniser but also disdain, as there are many things a foreigner does not understand.

– Down! Down!

Her lips shouted out the words, her hand rose in the air. The knife came down on the golden disc and split it in two. The letters of the name engraved on it flew in all directions like particles of sand. The armoured plate under the disc was also split in two. The blade of the knife cut into a piece of stone shaped like a heart and emerged from the other side, shining under the moonlight, spotlessly clean, without a trace of blood.

She hid her head under the eiderdown. She thought he was human with a body made of flesh and blood. But he was made of stone, a statue of the god Ra'a, or of King Ramses, which her father had received in exchange for the furnishings of the bridal house and the dowry.[1]

– Ganat.

She heard the voice of the Head Nurse calling out to her. She put her head out from under the eiderdown. The Head Nurse stood in front of her, clothed in her white uniform, her head swathed in a white veil. On her breast shone a golden disc with letters engraved on it. They were black and jagged like the legs of a black beetle: The Head Nurse.

She hid her head under the eiderdown.

[1] In the usual marriage system, when a daughter is married the father is responsible for furnishing the house into which the couple will move. The bridegroom's family pay the father of the girl a dowry and buy jewellery.

– Do you know who I am, Ganat?

– You are the Head Nurse.

– No, I am Narguiss.

– Narguiss who?

– Don't you remember me?

– No.

– We used to play hopscotch together.

– What hopscotch?

– Don't you remember our school?

– What school?

– And Sheikh Bassiouni?

– Which Sheikh?

– Don't you remember anything at all?

– No.

The Director could be seen sitting at his desk behind the glass panel. His body was enveloped in his white coat. His hair had all fallen out except for a white strand above the ears. His lips were parted in a smile exposing jagged yellow teeth. He took his pen out of his upper pocket and wrote on a long sheet of paper with worn edges: *Loss of memory indicating complete cure. To be discharged tomorrow before dawn.*

He folded the piece of paper four times, then remembered the stamp. No document could be authenticated without the stamp, without the circular piece of iron or zinc which had a handle like a hammer. The blacksmith cut it, then engraved it with the picture of the god Ra'a. On its face was a hooked nose like an eagle.

He held the hammer between his thumb and index finger, pursed his lips, closed his eyes, muttered in one breath: God, the King, Our Country, and brought the hammer down on the piece of paper. He handed it to the Head Nurse inside an envelope sealed with red wax.

The Head Nurse did not reach out to take the envelope. For thirty years she had reached out with her hand to take written orders from him. For thirty years she had stood with bent head, unable to lift her eyes to him.

She lifted her head and gazed into his eyes. They were bulging like those of her dead grandfather.

– What's the matter with you, girl? Why are you standing like a statue?

– My name is Narguiss, not girl.

– Since when?

He lifted his hand and brought his cane down on her breast.

– Since when, you girl?

– From now onwards.

– Prepare the beer and the snacks. I'm coming to see you tonight.

– I'm leaving, leaving everything.

– Where are you going? To another man?

– I hate you. I hate all men.

– You love women now, eh?

– Yes.

– You'll go to Hellfire with Lot's mother.

– No, sir, I won't.

– To be a lesbian is a sin, don't you know that?

– No, sir. It is not mentioned in God's book.

– You fallen woman. You whore.

He raised his hand higher up in the air so that it almost touched the ceiling. It came down on her face. The world turned one complete circle around her. The walls spun. The body of the Director went round with the earth. She could see him standing on his head with his legs held up in the air. The sky had collapsed on the earth. Police cars ran over it, their wheels turned upwards to the sky. The trams and the trains ran off the rails and capsized. The Pyramid of Khoufou stood on its tip with its base facing upwards. Whistles echoed, and bells rang, the bells of schools and the bells of churches. Sounds like bells ringing also came from the minarets. Military marches could be heard. Women cried out and their *you yous* of joy were like screams. The entreaties of beggars and the calls of newspaper vendors rose in the air. Loudspeakers and microphones shouted out from the walls and from the tops of columns. Then there were more military marches and the sound of rockets exploding. A red-coloured spray like droplets of rain filled the air. The smell of gunpowder and burning oil was everywhere. The air was heavy with smoke and a black fog filled the universe.

– You fallen woman. You whore.

The sound echoed behind her as she ran. Her feet swayed on high and tapering heels which hit the tiled floor with a sharp staccato voice. Her body was shaking. She almost fell over. She took off her shoes, threw them behind her back and ran barefoot along the corridor. Behind her the voice continued to echo in a long whistle that sounded like a thousand whistles in unison. She continued to run without stopping. The veil around her head came undone and the edges fluttered in the air. They twirled around her neck and started to choke her. She undid the veil from around her neck, slipped it off her head and threw it into the air. She unfastened the elastic corset from over her buttocks and let it fall down over her legs, then kicked it away.

– You whore.

The whistles echoed behind her as she ran on. Over her breast was the heavy golden disc which kept rising and falling with her panting breath. It rubbed against her breasts. She pulled on it with her fingers, undid the pin, and threw it away. She emptied her pockets of everything, the needle, the whistle, the coins, the reports. Slips of paper flew around her as she ran. Her body was getting lighter and lighter. Over her eyes formed a film of unshed tears. Thirty years of sadness. But under the surface there was a new gleam, like the eyes of another woman, happy to be free. She opened her arms and embraced the air. Her feet did not touch the ground. The way was open up in front of her as far as the horizon, endless spaces of green through which she ran, like a white butterfly. She clapped her wings and flew. By her side was another white butterfly. They hovered together in the air, laughed with the voices of children and embraced.

Suddenly there was an explosion like gunfire. The two butterflies dropped to the ground. The world went silent and the air was still. The heads of trees remained still. The sun dropped down near the horizon, descending from behind the clouds with a slow heavy movement. A green leaf shone under the light and shivered before it came to rest on the ground. Upon it fell one red drop after the other, slowly, drop by drop, as red as blood, with a slow beat, audible to the ears, beat after beat, in a regular rhythm like the beat of a heart.

11 *Nefissa Stops Calling Out*

She was lying in the female ward. The voice wafted over her closed eyelids like soft music. The bed beneath her swayed in a slow dance and the beating under her ribs echoed the same rhythmic movements. She was dancing in the wide-open green spaces that extended as far as the same music. Birds fluttered in the trees and chirped. The horse stamped on the ground with the rhythmic step of a military march. The goat went: Maa, maa, maa as though it were laughing. The cow stopped turning the water-wheel and guffawed with mirth, and the donkey lifted its head and hee-hawed so deeply that it seemed to be gasping for breath. The snake jutted its head out of a crack and its eyes shone with amusement. The rays of the sun danced on the waves of the Nile. The branches of the palm trees and the leaves on the trees trembled in the breeze, and the buds of the cotton trees burst into bolls and covered the land with white surf. When she sang, her voice hovered over her head in circles of silver. Her bare feet beat down on the earth. Her breasts and her shoulders moved with her arms and her legs, and the brass castanets rang between her fingers.

– Your love is like a fire, my darling. Like a fire, my love! A fire!

Her voice echoed in her ears. It resembled that of her Aunt Zanouba. In the village they called Aunt Zanouba El Alma![1] In the night she used to hear her grandfather whisper:

– O God thou who knowest all things.

During the day she saw her Aunt Zanouba sitting amongst the men. She smoked the water pipe and blew the smoke into the Headman's face. The Headman threw his head back and laughed, and the men around him called her El Alma. Her house was built of red brick. It rose two storeys higher than the house of the Headman, and was three metres higher than the House of God.[2] She moved her arms and legs freely in front of the Headman. She feared no one, not the King, nor the President, nor the General. She stamped on the ground and her voice rose in song. Everyone acclaimed her name and called her Zanouba El Alma. Their eyes gleamed and their irises trembled in the whites of their eyes. Their hearts beat under their ribs and in their hearts was hidden a feeling like

---

[1] *El Alma* means the one who knows, who has a vast and deep knowledge of things. It also means a woman dancer.
[2] The mosque.

awe, a fear mingled with lust. She knew their secrets. She knew what was hidden, what was beyond ordinary understanding. God had revealed things to her. She read the cup[1] and the palm of the hand. She could decode the signs in the palm and understand the language of shells. She mingled with spirits and sirens, and on the wedding night she it was who made sure that the white towel was soaked in blood, even if the bride had been a widow for one or two centuries.[2]

– Like a burning fire, my love! My love! A burning fire!

At night she dreamt that she had become like her Aunt Zanouba. She walked with a tall, slim body, her head held upright, looking people straight in the face with wide-open eyes. Her eyes were never lowered to the ground, her back was never bent. Her voice echoed in the air like a *you you* of joy. It made the women *you you* in turn, made men laugh and feel happy. The sun came out from behind the clouds at the sound of her voice, and the world became full of light. Her voice was as tender as that of her mother when she called out to her.

– Nefissa!

The name echoed strangely in her ears, as she lay under the bank of the river. It was as though she were

[1] Telling a person's fortune from the dregs left in a coffee cup.
[2] Meant as sarcasm. The girl could have no hymen but El Alma could stain the towel with other blood.

hearing the name of another woman being called out. It went through her ears. She clapped her hands over them and hit her head. It was not her mother's voice calling out, nor was it that of her Aunt Zanouba. It was a hoarse, guttural voice, like that of the Head of the village guards.

– Nefissa!

She opened one eye and peered out. The Headman of the Village was walking along the bank of the river. He was wearing a velvet *caftan*. Over his head he wore a white veil tied around his neck with a black belt. He was accompanied by guards and soldiers carrying guns. They addressed him as *Your Majesty*. He trod the ground with a slow, solemn step, his head held upright, with the drums beating. Under his arm he carried the Book of God. He walked slowly up to the platform, bowed down and shook hands with El Khawaga, the General, who wore a military uniform and a belt around his waist. His face was white and square like the face of a bear. His cheeks were swollen with air, and under his arm he carried the Bible.

The national anthem was playing. Lights converged on the two faces standing on the platform. The magnesium flares lit up with a white light. A small muscle trembled under the right eye of His Majesty. The head of the General was up in the air and sat steadfast on his neck like the Sphinx. He watched His Majesty out of the corner of his eye as he took the Book of God from under his arm, and opened it using his thumb and index finger to turn the pages. He read the verse of Eblis and closed it, kissed the book first on the front then on the back, put it under his arm again, and looked at the General out of the corner of his eye. The General pulled the Bible from under his arm and turned the pages with his thumb and index finger, read out the verse of Eblis, closed it and put it under his arm without kissing it.

The band struck up a military march. The General declared war. He made a long speech in a foreign language. His Majesty translated it into Arabic which made it even more confusing. He kept repeating a word the people had not heard before, pronouncing the syllables separately.

– Za-Di-fil.[1]

The village people looked at one another. One of them whispered into the ear of his neighbour:

– Does he mean the *phil*[2] at the zoo?

But the General corrected the word. He stuck his white tongue out between his lips and pronounced:

– The Devil!

His Majesty did not know how to put the tip of his tongue between his lips. He pressed his lips together tightly and looked up at the sky with humility. The Khawaga declared war, and made a speech about

---

[1] The Devil.
[2] *Phil* in Arabic means elephant.

peace in a foreign language. His Majesty translated it into Arabic which made it even more confusing.

The village people looked at one another. Their eyes were half-closed. The noise of their snoring as they slept could be heard louder than any other sound. They opened their eyes when the singing began and the castanets clicked out the rhythm of the love dance.

– Your love is a burning fire! Fire! Fire!

They nodded their heads and swayed their bodies, shouting with one voice.

– Fire, my love, fire!

All of them were shouting loudly and all of them were silent. The silence echoed in her ears like the roar of a waterfall, and the roar of the waterfall seemed to change into a prolonged, faint sound like someone quietly weeping. She ran in the dark, holding her hands over her buttocks. The cane hissed through the air and stung her back time after time. Red marks showed on her naked flesh. They curled and twisted like the tails of serpents. The voice of Sheikh Masoud bellowed:

– Recite the verse of Eblis, girl.

She ran with her back to him and her face to the wind. She hid from the eyes of people in the cloak of the night, and took the train from the village to the city. Her body shook with the movement of the train. The wheels clattered over the rails, and the broken windows responded with crackling noises. She sat on a wooden bench carrying a cotton bag on her knees. Her black hair flew around her in the air. The train whistled and smoke filled her nose and her mouth. Waves of yellow light moved over the pale faces, and yellow eyes stared at her breasts. She lifted the satchel in front of them. Opposite her was a small girl who was at school with her. She was wearing an orange-coloured uniform with small squares and a white collar high around the neck. She looked at her with shining eyes. It was the first time she had travelled on a train and seen the houses and the trees run backwards. Her heart beat under her ribs to the rhythm of the wheels. Her voice rang out above the sound of the wheels:

– What's your name?

– Ganat.

She pronounced *Ganat* with a voice that was like singing, as soft as a ray of sunlight in winter, then threw her hair back and laughed. Her laughter rose in the air like circles of silver. On her knees was an exercise book with a green cover. Its paper was fine, almost transparent. There were letters written with a pen over its lines and she chanted line after line in a voice that was like the whisper of a breeze:

– I am Ganat.

Its root is *Ginan*.

It is the plural of *Gana*.

It is rare for a flower to grow in the desert.

I am a jewel.

The earth looked at the sky, and the chanting voice flowed through her veins like a stream of blood. The pride of just one of her own sex was enough. She filled her lungs with air, threw back her head and laughed. She too hovered in the heavens like a dove, fluttered her wings, and danced.

– What are you dreaming of, Nefissa?

– I want to be an *Alima*.[1]

She could see her write her name, *Ganat the poetess*, on the stones of the Pyramids, and next to her she wrote, *Nefissa the dancer*. She put one foot on the Pyramid, lifted the other in the air, and flew over the city. She wanted nothing from the world except to dance, to be able to move her arms and legs in the air, to create her own dance and not that of her aunt Zanouba, to engrave her own name, and no other name, even the name of the King. She did not want to be the wife of the Headman or the esteemed spouse of the President or of the King. She wanted to be Nefissa the Greatest of *Alimas*, radiating in the sky like the morning star, leaving her own stamp on the world. She wanted to play music, to dance.

– I am the planet Zahra.

Forever in the sky.

I do not fade or fall.

---

[1] Meaning dancer in the sense given previously for the word *El Alma* (she who knows).

I am Nefissa, the daughter of my mother, the Sad One.

Under the glow of happiness her eyes would fill with tears. She could see her mother standing in the darkness. Her back was towards her, her face to the window. She stood upright like that all through the night. Her head never fell forwards on her breast. She slept standing up. Her voice wept softly all night.

– Where is my son, o Zahra, mother of justice and compassion?

The voice floated over her eyelids as she lay on the mat. She stretched out her arm as far as she could. It hit the wall. His place by her side was empty. The emptiness stretched out to the whole universe. He slept with his arm under his head as a pillow. His hair was thick and black. His breath smelt like children. Fine hairs had started to grow on his upper lip. His skin was dark, as dark as hers, and his fingers were like hers, long and tapering. His lips were slightly open and his eyes closed. He turned over on the other side, and the cover dropped off his back. Her mother's hand crept out in the darkness and covered him. The wind blew in the distance with a howling noise like a wolf. The leaves fell from the trees. Particles of sand and dust and smoke filled the air like a mist. Raindrops beat on the windows. She stretched her neck out from under the covers. The wind dropped and the rain ceased. It was like a silence before the storm. Something fearful from the unknown yet to come. Her chest rose and fell and her ears were strained to listen.

She heard the knocking at the door, and an iron heel stamped on the ground. The voice of the Head Guard cut through the silence, hoarse and guttural like the voice of Sheikh Masoud.

– Where is Eblis?

He nudged her shoulder with his elbow as she lay on the mat.

– Where is your brother, girl?

He kicked her in the stomach with the tip of his boot. She caught hold of a stone and threw it at him. It hit him in the eye. They rushed at her like a swarm of locusts, carried her to the armoured car. She could see her face in the mirror. It was long and pale like the face of her mother. A yellow rosary hung from the mirror, and on the shelf in front of the steering wheel was a gilt-edged Koran in a box lined with green velvet, and another box with pink paper tissues. She pulled out a tissue and wiped away her sweat. The driver looked at her out of the corner of his eye. His head under the brass helmet was shaven. He pressed a black button with his finger and a coarse voice began to chant the Koran.

– *And thy God did say: I shall appoint a viceroy on the earth. And they asked: Shalt thou appoint him who will sow evil and shed blood?*

He pressed another button and a woman's voice burst out singing:

– Burning fire, my love, burning fire!

He nodded his head and sang with her:

– Burning fire, my love, burning fire!

He stretched out his arm towards her as she sat close up against the door, curled up around herself, inside a white cotton gown, her hair tied tight with a white ribbon.

She felt his finger run up her left leg, smooth as the tail of a snake. It crept over her knee, but before it could go higher her hand moved out and gripped it. With her other hand she slipped off her shoe. It was an old leather shoe with a thick, square heel. She took it off without undoing the laces. It was too big for her foot. Her brother used to take it off, then take the other one off as well and walk barefoot to school. She would walk barefoot beside him but the hot ground would burn her soles. So when he took off one shoe he gave it to her. She would hop on the foot with the shoe and keep the other foot off the ground. He played hopscotch with her, with one foot bare, and the other shod like her. They jumped together and the children around them laughed.

The laughter which rose from her as she jumped on the ground with one foot continued to echo in her ears. She lifted the other foot in the air and beat down with it on the ground, one beat after the other in rhythm with the *tabla*.[1] The beating of her heart quickened with the rhythm of the dance.

– Lub dib, lib dib, lib dib.

– I am Nefissa, the daughter of my mother Sadness. My Aunt Zanouba is the star of our village.

The music and the beating suddenly stopped and there was a deep silence. Her face was pale, drained of its blood. The sun hid behind a mist like smoke. The face of Sheikh Masoud peered out of it. She could hear the hiss of the cane as it cut through the air, feel the air sting the flesh of her bare buttocks. Red marks showed up on her body. They twisted and writhed like the tails of serpents.

She was standing with her face to the wall and her back to him. She had never been able to turn round and look at him face to face. This time she did. Under the brass helmet she saw the face. It was square and white, the colour of death. He had swollen, fleshy jowls. His shoulders were squeezed into the military uniform, and a tin disc shone dully on his chest.

She threw her shoe at him and opened the door of the car. She jumped out, running on her bare feet in the dark. She hid in the shadows of the trees as she ran, lifting her robe around her breasts, stifling her breath till she almost choked herself as she stood leaning against the trunk of a tree.

[1] A special long-necked, hollow-sounding drum used for Oriental dances.

She could hear the beating under her ribs. She pressed her hand to her heart. The moonlight fell on him as he walked towards her. His shadow showed long and dark over the ground. His head was thick and square under the brass helmet. His shoes were iron shod. They crushed the green plants growing on the earth. She could hear the sound of leaves crackling under his weight. The Khamaseen winds howled in the distance like wolves. Dust filled the air like a fog. She lifted her face to the Heavens.

– O God.

No one in the Heavens answered her cry as she ran on alone in the dark. The wind blew away the white ribbon tied to hold her hair. It lifted her robe up to her waist. She pulled it down to hide her belly, and her eyes looked up at the morning star and called out to her mother. But her mother had died in the village, and her brother had been taken away before the sun rose out of the night. She walked along the river bank, with her eyes closed and her arms stretched out. Around her neck was a fine chain with a tiny Koran attached to it. The street along the Nile was enveloped in the shade of eucalyptus trees. A big houseboat floated close to the bank. The neon lights shone white on the river waters. Laughter resounded in the night and with it the click of brass castanets.

– Burning fire, my love, burning fire.

The smell of grilled meat filled her nose. She sat on

the shore inhaling the odour of food that rose up to her. Close by was the road with cars sweeping past. Headlight after headlight slid over her face as she sat there. Her face appeared, disappeared, then appeared again, time after time, a pale yellow blob, then black, then a yellow blob again. Her wide-open eyes stared into the light, two dark circles as black as the night, burning with hunger.

On the pavement lay a girl enveloped in a black robe. She was curled up around herself like a child in its womb. Between her arms she held a baby which sucked at her breast. A new-born kitten fed at the other breast. A dustbin lay on its side, and a puppy gnawed at a small bone. It ran off, limping on three legs, then lifted a hind leg and urinated on the wall.

She got up and walked to the dustbin with a limping step. The puppy watched her with a sad, broken look and over its eyes crept a film of moisture. The pupil trembled but the tear did not fall out. It left the bone to her and crept up close. She caressed its head and pushed the small bone back to it. She brought her mouth close to its ear and whispered. The puppy sniffed at her neck and touched the silver chain play-fully with its paw. Her breast rose and fell under the robe, and the gilt-edged Koran shook. She pulled at the chain and clenched it between her teeth.

She walked down to the door of the houseboat. Through the glass she could see pieces of meat roasting on a spit. A man was moving a feather fan over the fire as though chasing away flies. She stretched out her hand, holding the gilt-edged Koran to him. He held it between his thumb and index finger, looked at one side and then at the other, rang it down on the marble top, and then put it on one pan of the scales. In the other pan he put a piece of meat.

She walked near the wall, chewing the meat. The puppy limped behind her. She gave him a small piece. He took hold of it between his little teeth and wagged his tail. He lifted his hind leg and urinated on the wall. The wall was high and on top of it there were decorations and flags, and a picture of Zanouba, near-naked in her flimsy dancer's dress, beating on the ground with one bare foot. When she danced the earth shook, the chairs on the earth shook, the bodies sitting in the chairs on the earth shook, the shaven heads shook. The hats and turbans and skullcaps, and the Arab head-dresses and fezzes and dunce caps worn when people celebrate, and the coloured masks of carnivals, all fell off. In the middle was a gilt chair with a high back. The face was square and white, and on the head was a conical cap topped by a feather. Behind him stood a tall black slave wearing dark glasses. Zanouba lifted one leg in the air and beat down on the ground with the other foot. The feather shook and below it the conical cap. The slave reached out with both hands and steadied it carefully on the head.

A circle of light moved with Zanouba. Her breasts showed naked under the dancer's dress. On each breast was a small circular bead, black in colour. Her legs were long and slim and tense, curving upwards to her belly. Around her navel was a circle of tiny blue beads and on her forehead she wore a red golden disc. Her eyes were two pools of glowing fire. She stamped on the ground like a lioness.

– Burning fire, my love, burning fire.

The high-backed chair was shaking fast, and the conical cap fell off before the black servant had time to steady it on the head. The wind blew it away like a balloon. It hovered over the garden for a while, flew over the high wall, blew up and then dropped on to the river bank.

The puppy ran up to it and took hold of it between its teeth. The other stray dogs collected around, and the children stood watching with wide-open eyes swarming with flies. The canes landed on their naked buttocks and a man shouted at them:

– You boy, and you, push off!

His voice resembled the Head Guard's, and the shore looked like the river bank in the village. But the street was paved with black tarmac, and neon lights hung from high posts, and on every post was a picture, the same picture with the same face that looked out of the gilt-edged frame. The square shape of the head resembled the square head of King Ramses, and it had two horns curving down in front like those of the god Ra'a.

– Nefissa!

The name rang out over her closed eyelids. It sounded strange and yet familiar to her ears. It was like her name. She hid her head under the cotton eiderdown. It was covered in red satin, and the pillowcase was white with black stains the colour of kohl. Around her eyes were lines painted with an eye pencil. They were washed away at night by sweat, and a fine thread of clear water that flowed out of the corner of her eye. Her breasts were squeezed inside an elastic bra, and around each breast was a chain of beads. Her lips were coloured with red paint, and on each cheek was a circular stain like blood.

– Nefissa, o Nefissa.

Daughter of Eblissa

You ignite fire

You are in every heart.

She hid from them under the covers. She did not have to open her eyes to know their faces. Their heads were shaven and smelt of cologne. Their chins were smooth and well shaven. Their breath smelt of burnt oil. They hid their eyes behind dark glasses and sat in the waiting-room licking their lips. The hairs on their noses stood up, and trembled in the air like the whiskers of cats smelling roast meat. They mewed under her hands in pain, and they bit into the back of her neck with their teeth, as though biting on a piece of meat. They filled her ears with dirty words.

– You whore, you fallen woman.

She blocked her ears with cotton wool. She carried their load of guilt, and the guilt grew under her ribs like a swelling. They paid her the price of the medicine with which she treated them, and added enough for her daughter's supper that night. She raised her face to the Heavens and spoke to God: O God . . . Whoever saw her thought she was speaking to herself. The stick prodded her shoulder.

– It's forbidden to speak to God, Nefissa!

– God does not speak to females, Nefissa!

– You're a runaway from the cage, you, Nefissa!

She escaped in the dark of night. She did not know where to go. Even God was owned by them. They built houses for him with concrete and bricks. They imprisoned him between high walls or in stone engravings, or between leather covers, and lines of print, or in letters moulded out of lead. She could not read, nor did she have the money to buy books. So sin after sin collected under her ribs, and grew into something she felt like a heart. She carried it in her breast like a child and walked day and night. She slept as she walked, her eyes on the road which stretched to the end of the shore, to her mother's village. The smell of milk and baking bread. The particles of dust and dung. Her mother's long dress curled up on the mud oven, smelling of blood. On the ground the leaves of a dead tree. An exercise book, its edges eaten away by moths. The soul of her grandfather standing near the water-closet. A basket of dried bread covered in flies. A shoe, the one she wore to school. Her brother's *gallabeya* hanging from a rusty nail in the wall, lifting in the air and shivering with a voice which whispered:

– Nefissa.

Her eyes rose up towards the ceiling. The snake peered out from a crack. Its eyes filled with tears. The cow stopped turning the water-wheel, and sobbed in a low voice. The donkey raised its head up and wiped its sweat with its foreleg. Tears of blood dropped from the leaves of the trees like drops of rain.

She walked on, her eyes dry, staring ahead. The air was heavy, saturated with smoke and defeat, with the smell of gunpowder and burning oil. People walked over the pavements with closed eyes, their mouths open, their breath coming in gasps. The crowds were dense and bodies were hemmed up against each other in long columns and lines that stretched out as far as the horizon. They made a way for themselves with flailing arms and legs, fought with their heads like goats. They lifted the palms of their hands to the skies. Flat loaves of bread fell from above, round and hot, and flushed like the sun, crackling with heat from the oven, flying over their heads like balloons. The lines were broken, and the columns became crooked. There was confusion and chaos with people rushing here and there. The canes rained down on their backs.

– Order! Order![1]

The voices sounded in her ears like the whistle of the wind, and the whistle was like a thousand whistles, like a thousand voices shouting: The system, the system,[2] and a thousand voices gasped: Down! Down! Everyone was shouting and everyone was silent.

She opened her mouth as wide as she could and screamed, but no sound came out. Her chest was tied with a band of leather like a belt. On her feet she wore a pair of open shoes, which displayed her toenails varnished in red. Her heels clicked over the tarmac road with a loud noise.

– Tak, tak, tak, tak, tak.

The sound came from behind her. A woman was following her. Her steps on the ground made the same rhythmic sound. Her shadow appeared beside her, and followed her step by step. Her dress was the same black colour, her breasts naked under the moonlight.

She turned round and looked behind her. The woman hid behind a wall, or a lamppost. She moved away and walked on. She could hear steps behind her once again. She stopped in the middle of the bridge. She could feel breath on her neck, hear panting with a sound like quick sobs.

[1] and [2] In Arabic the same word, *Nizam*, is used to mean both order and the system.

She opened her small bag. It was black and covered with shining beads. She took out a paper tissue and dried a drop of sweat on her nose.

She continued on without looking round, and almost reached the end of the bridge, but the sobbing still came from behind her. Her body came to a stop. She leaned over the parapet and gazed at the surface of the water. It was shining like a mirror under the moonlight. The mirror moved in small circles over its surface, then became still again, shining in the white light. Little waves ran over it with a lazy movement raised by slow shifts of wind.

She could see her floating on the waves, surrounded by green plants called Flowers of the Nile. Her dress was black and her breasts were naked. Her face looked up at the sky and her lips were moving as though she were talking to God.

The world suddenly went silent, and the wind ceased its movement. The heads of the trees shed immobile shadows on the ground. The moon hid behind a black mist of smoke and soot. The faces of people were the colour of dust, and their eyes were closed. They breathed through open mouths with a sound like stifled sobs.

Millions of quiet sobs rose in the air with each particle of dust. The waters of the Nile shrank rapidly down to the bottom and their surface was covered with dark weeds like dead bodies, thousands of bodies which carried flags and banners of victory. The neon lamps reflected their lights on the surface of the water. Shapes floated on it. They looked like sleeping bodies with heads in which there were dark, open cavities. They looked at the sky silently, made no sound, said nothing, showed no despair, no hope, nothing. All around was just a white light like snow which covered the surface of the moon, a sad, silent light like that in her mother's eyes when they stared into space without regret, or hope, or expectation of any kind, just a long, continuous stare which came from nowhere and was going nowhere.

12 *Ganat Breaks Out*

That night the clouds were black and heavy. The air was loaded with smoke and defeat. The huge door opened, its hinges creaking like an ancient water-wheel. It was an unexpected sound in the complete silence that usually reigned. The walls of the palace trembled visibly. The heads of the trees shed their dark shadows on the ground. A branch bent over and broke, and a bird sitting on its eggs fell out of its nest and disappeared into the dark horizon. The shells of the eggs were scattered over the ground, and small chicks looked out, their heads shivering in the cold.

A movement went through the bodies lying in the ward, human bodies, sons of Adam and daughters of Eve. Their eyes, half-closed in what looked like sleep, opened wide, and within them lay an imprisoned tear which neither dried nor fell out. Their robes were white, the colour of shrouds, and their pupils were as black as the night, staring into space in a kind of daze.

She was lying in a coffin which was being carried on people's shoulders, wearing a long robe the colour of a wedding dress. The flounces flew around her like wings. The box swayed over the bodies in a rhythmic dance, like a baby's cot, or a child's swing. Her wide-open eyes looked upwards, and her lips were parted in a smile. She was singing, in a quiet voice, what sounded like an old melody:

– I am Ganat which comes from *Ginan* and is the plural of *Gana*.

I am Zahra.

It's rare for a flower to blossom in the desert.

I am not the Virgin Mary, nor am I Eve the Wicked.

I am not a whore and I am not a pure, virtuous woman.

I am a human being and my heart is my God.

My crime was a poem.

Under the white shroud which covered her body in the box her breast rose and fell. To it was pinned a slip of paper. It was stamped with the horns of the Ibis calf, and the beak of the eagle. It was her official death certificate. Her triple name was written on it in black ink in the handwriting of the Director. The letters were jagged, and crooked like the legs of beetles moving under a glass bell.

– Ganat Abd Allah Abdil Illah.[1]

[1] Ganat, slave of God, slave of the God.

Her eyes opened wide and the pupils grew bigger and bigger. It was as though she were seeing her triple name for the first time. Abdallah?! Who was Abdallah? Was it her father's name? Abdil Illah? Was it her grandfather's name? Her memory awakened little by little. Her grandmother's voice echoed in her ears like a whistle. She was calling her grandfather *Abdil Illat*,[1] changing the *h* into *t*. Her grandfather almost jumped out of his high-backed chair.

– *Abdil Illah* not *Abdillat*.

Her grandmother opened her mouth wide, took a long, deep breath and expelled it slowly. She stuck out her tongue between parted lips to pronounce the letter properly, but it seemed to twist from her and change the *h* into *t*.

– *Abdillat*.

Her grandfather waved his wrinkled, blue-veined hand excitedly in the air and shouted:

– *Illah* not *Illat*!

He held her grandmother's sinewy hand in his, made her write the letter *h* in the form of a round cake, in a circle without two dots, and then the *t* the same, only with two dots over the circle.

– The feminine has two dots on it.

From under the eiderdown where she lay she could

---

[1] *Illat* in the Arab peninsula was a female goddess before Islam. Her name was written in the same way as Illah, the monotheistic Islamic god, but two dots are added to the last letter.

hear her grandmother repeat the same mistake. She forgot to put the two dots on the round cake. Her grandfather's voice resounded in the night.

– The two dots, you she-ass!

The word *she-ass* stung her ears like the blow of a cane. Ever since her father had deprived her of the family inheritance her husband had started to call her a she-ass. Before that he used to address her as *lady mistress*. The brass posts of the bed began to shake, her breast rose and fell, and her breath came in gasps. Her voice growled with a sound like air trying to break out from an enclosed space:

– Making a history out of two dots.

  Turning the world upside down just because of two dots.

  God take you from this world.

She made the sign of the cross over her chest and muttered:

– Our Father which art in Heaven, forgive us our trespasses.

She closed her eyes, then half-opened one eye and glimpsed her grandmother lying by her side staring at the ceiling.

– Go to sleep, Ganat. Why are you awake?

– Is Father called Abdallah, Nena?

– Yes.

– And grandfather Abdil Illah?

– Go to sleep, Ganat, and try to overcome the Devil.

– Is Allah[1] other than Al Illah?[2]

– I don't know. Ask your father and your grandfather.

In the morning her father went out before she could ask him. Her grandfather told her that Allah was the same as Al Illah. He protruded the tip of his tongue and opened his jaws as wide as he could pronouncing a very long *a* after the double *l* in Illah. With the name Allah he filled his cheeks with air, and stuck his tongue to his palate.

– Is Al Illah the same as Allah, Grandfather?

He opened his eyes wide and gave her a sharp look. It was the first time she had seen the colour of the iris in her grandfather's eyes. It was black, pitch black, and in the middle was a small hole like the mouth of a pit. His face was square with a white complexion, and above the upper lip he had white whiskers cut in a neat square. His teeth were big and yellow with jagged edges, and his voice was guttural with a hoarseness which showed at the end of his sentences.

– I take refuge in thee, o God, from the sinful Devil.

He held her small fingers in his big hand. He made her write the sentence three times in her homework copy book. The tip of the pen moved over the white paper: *I take refuge in thee, o God, . . . I take refuge in . . .*, but the pen went dry in the middle of the word. She filled it up from the inkpot, and finished the word,

[1] Allah means God.
[2] Al Illah means the God.

drawing the *h* like a round cake as her mother had taught her to do. She lifted the pen from the paper after closing the circle of the *h*. The tip of the pen was as thin as a needle and a drop of ink fell off it above the round cake. Before she had time to move her pen, a second drop fell off next to it. The *h* had been turned into a *t*.

It was as though the world had been overturned. Sheikh Bassiouni gazed at her copy book. His body shook, and his teeth chattered.

– *I take refuge in Al Illah! I take refuge in Al Illah!*

He stung her with the cane three times over each fingertip. Then he grasped the rubber in his hand and started to rub off the two dots from over the *h* with a repressed fury. He pressed down on the rubber with the full weight of his body until he tore the paper. The two dots disappeared but with them also the round cake of the *h*.

He walked between the desks staring at the copy books of the girls. Every time his eyes saw two dots his body shook, and his teeth chattered as though he were seeing Eblis in person, and not two dots of ink. The hiss of the stick descending in the air could be heard each time, followed by a rubbing noise as he erased the two dots as though forever banishing the face of the Devil from the earth.

He squatted on the chair with the book open in front of him. He wetted his finger with saliva and turned the pages. He stopped at a page and started to read in a loud voice, and the girls repeated what he said in unison.

– *And dids't thou witness Illat and El Ouza and Manat[1] who is their third. And shalt thou have the male, and he the female. That is indeed an unjust way to apportion them out.*

He swallowed his saliva making a loud noise in his throat. His Adam's apple rose up in his gullet, then dropped. He stared at the girls from behind his spectacles as they sat at their desks, their faces pale, their heads swathed in white gauze, their eyes looking at the ground with lowered lids, and their mouths open. He landed his fist violently on the wooden table.

– Attention!

Then he went on reading.

– *Those who do not believe in the forever after do call the angels by female names.*

The word *female* rang in her ears as though she were hearing it for the first time. He pouted his lips as he pronounced the *f* and the *m* in *female*. His lips formed a round opening as though preparing to spit. He wiped his mouth with the back of his sleeve.

There was a deep silence in the class. The girls shrank behind their desks. He closed the book and

[1] Three female gods who had statues in Mecca and were worshipped by Arabs before Islam. *He* here refers to God.

stood up. He walked between the rows blinking his eyes. He moved his nose between their heads, sniffing like a cat. The hairs in his nostrils stood out stiffly. His lips were parted and he muttered in a quiet voice which sounded like a hiss in the air.

– The female . . . the female.

He stuck out his lips as he pronounced the word, his teeth clenching at the end with the threat of something to come. He closed his eyes and yawned, then opened one eye. The pupil, small and round, seemed to turn round on itself, vibrating like a black marble as it fixed itself on the small breasts rising and falling under the school uniforms.

The girls folded their arms over their breasts, pressed their knees tightly together, and shrank into their bodies. They hid their heads under their desks and gasped as though stifling their sobs.

He stopped beside her as she sat with her back straight up, her hands on her desk, her eyes wide open in an unblinking look.

He stung her on her hand with his cane.

– Lower your lids, girl!

Bend your Head!

Do not raise your eyes and look at me like that.

Her eyes were wide open and they always looked up. Her mother's voice had echoed in her ears since the day she was born, like an old song that flowed with the blood through her veins, a song the words of which were etched on a piece of paper in dark lines that showed up in the moonlight:

– I have no fear of you who fight against knowledge and close our eyes so that we should not see.

I have no fear.

The cane kept landing on her hands and arms. She could hear it hiss through the air, but felt no pain, could see the red marks on her flesh writhing like serpents' tails. A drop of blood fell on to the tiled floor, and shone like a golden disc. She wiped it away with the heel of her shoe and raised her head. She walked between the rows of girls and boys, her body tall and slim. They carried her on their shoulders, her head touching the sky. She set her foot on the top of the Pyramid of Khoufou and shouted out loud:

– Down with Sheikh Bassiouni.

Down with the King, and the British.

Down! Down! Down!

The streets filled with people. Women came out of the houses and lanes. The doors of the schools opened and people poured out. Children wearing aprons, and young people, boys and girls. Old people who tapped on the ground with their sticks. Men and women, their faces wrinkled, their eyes like grey marbles trembling behind glass. The cat which had abandoned the dustbin came running up, followed by the small puppy with a limp, and stray dogs. The infants lying on the pavements in their mothers' arms, and the beggars, and the newspaper vendors, and the soldiers standing like wooden posts with their faces to the wall, and the prostitutes wandering around in the night with chalked faces, and the people waiting in front of the bakeries, their bodies hemmed up against each other, forming long lines which extended further than the eye could see. The shouting in her ears was like the roar of a waterfall which kept on echoing:

– Down! Down! Down!

As she lay in the box she felt it shake. She lifted the lid and looked out. She saw the box being carried on shoulders like a boat in the sea. It slid over the waves to the rhythm of the song. The cries of the people were like a whispering wind. The dawn crept over the sky and the colours of the sun burst out.

– Down! Down! Down!

She rested her head on the pillow and closed her eyes. On her lips was a smile. The voice floated over her closed lids like a ray of sun, like the voice of her mother before she was born. It penetrated the wall of the womb as warm as the flow of blood.

Then the voice ceased. There was silence. The wind whistled in the distance, a long whistle like a horn. It cut through the silence like a gunshot. The shots rang out one after the other in rapid succession. Police whistles sounded all around, church bells rang loudly, microphones on lighthouses and minarets clamoured, tanks rolled out over the ground, iron heels stamped on the tarmac roads, and soldiers wearing brass helmets marched in line after line, after line, until thousands of lines had passed by.

She saw him emerge from the front row. She recognized him at once. He was wearing the white coat of the Director, and the body of her grandfather, and the hooked nose of Zakaria, and the square white face of the King, and the turban of Sheikh Bassiouni with the long feather standing in the air at the top.

She stood in front of him wearing her school apron. Around her neck was a white collar, and under her arm she held the pen and an exercise book.

He sat in the high-backed chair, on a throne of gold. Around him were his servants and his followers. His wife was sitting amongst the wives of his followers and they were called *El Hareem*.[1] Over his chest was a medal which shone. In front of him was a wooden table on which he rapped with a steel hammer, and in his mouth was a whistle on which he blew.

– The court is in session.

His voice resounded loudly in the compound around the palace. The doors of the wards opened wide. The men came out wrapped in their wide white robes. Around their waists were belts tied in a bow. On their feet were open rubber slippers called

[1] Literally means someone protected, not to be violated or touched because she belongs to someone else.

zanouba.[1] Their faces were pale, the colour of the clouds, their eyes wide open staring into space. They walked at a crawling pace. They crowded into the bare garden surrounded by a high wall. The women huddled together in a corner called the *harim*. Their heads were enveloped in grey veils, their faces long and thin with skin the colour of dust. They squatted on the ground with their eyes closed.

– The court is in session.

The eyes looked at him through a film of water like glass. His jaws opened and closed like scissors, and drops of saliva like particles of sand flew out of his mouth. One particle flew out and burst in the air. The air filled with the smell of shaving cream and petrol. He put on his spectacles and opened the book. He eyed people from behind his glasses, then blew on his whistle.

– In the name of God (he pronounced *God* like a shot from a gun).

– In the name of his sovereignty (his pronounciation became even more cutting).

– In the name of justice, honour, our religious jurisprudence, and international law (he pronounced the whole sentence in one breath).

– Gentlemen (he stared at the men from behind his glasses).

– Ladies (he bent his head, lowered his voice and

[1] A cheap slipper worn by poor people, also a sign of negligence.

took a quick look at his wife out of the corner of his eye as she sat in the corner of the *harim*.

– In the name of Allah the All-Merciful and the Compassionate.

– We open this session.

He held out an envelope sealed with red wax, and waved it above the table. He opened it with a long penknife, and a long white sheet of paper protruded from it. He brought it close to his face until it touched his nose, called out to her in her triple name as registered on the death certificate.

– Ganat Abdallah Abdil Illah.

The name echoed strangely in her ears, as though it were the name of another woman. She pressed her lips firmly together and was silent.

He pointed to her with his finger, all the time holding the whistle between his lips.

– This woman, gentlemen (he dropped *and ladies*), has been afflicted with a dangerous malady since the day she was born. An inherited madness, gentlemen, has run in her blood, coming down from her grandmother Eve. The signs of this sickness are as follows:

Firstly: Her eyes were wide open from the moment of her birth.

Secondly: Her face has remained uncovered even though she is no longer a minor and has attained the age of full responsibility.

Thirdly: Allying herself with Satan to overthrow the universal order.

Fourthly: Infringing on the laws of our religious jurisprudence and international legality.

He stared at the faces before him through his spectacles and was silent. Their eyelids were closed and their mouths half-open as they sat there sound asleep, wrapped in their white robes with a thin belt tied around the waist. Their breathing was loud as though they were almost snoring.

He rapped with the hammer on the table. The earth trembled and with it the bodies sitting on it. They opened their eyes and stared into space. Then their heads bent again and they plunged back into sleep.

He rapped on the table again. The earth and the bodies trembled, but no one awoke. He looked at the Chairman of the session out of the corner of his eye, and then turned his whole body round towards him until he was almost facing him.

– Your Majesty. The most dangerous of symptoms is for there to be no loss of memory despite electric shocks, repeated almost without interval, and injections considered lethal to the centres of memory in the brain, and threatening with Hellfire or tempting with Heaven. We did all that, Your Sovereignty, but to no avail. She remembers everything that has happened for five thousand years. She even remembers what happened long before that when the serpent whispered to Eblis, and when Eblis was still a virtuous and pure angel who knew nothing about corruption or evil.

He was silent for a long moment then stared into the face of His Majesty. He saw him sitting with closed eyes and open mouth, deep in sleep. A thin thread of white saliva dropped down from the corner of his mouth, down his chin. He blew his whistle and announced the end of the session. The male nurses appeared wearing their white aprons. They tied her arms and legs with ropes. They laid her in the box clothed in her wedding dress. They put a bouquet of flowers in her hands. They carried her on their shoulders and walked out into the road.

Over her eyelids she heard a voice like whispering, like a soft breeze, like the voice of her mother singing her to sleep as she rocked the cradle, like a warm ray of sun moving over her closed eyelids.

– I am Ganat and it comes from *Ginan* the plural of *Gana*.

I am a flower.

Flowers rarely blossom in the desert.

You who fight against history and put out the light.

You who are only yourself when you talk in riddles.

So that when you are clear, your words turn to nonsense.

I am not one or two dots in your book.

I am not a deleted name or the dash of a '*t*'.

I am not afraid.

You who shed blood and sow corruption on the earth.

You who hold a stick and demand obedience.

I do not hide my face. I am not ashamed of my body.

I do not put kohl around my eyes or carry someone else's name.

You who fight reason and knowledge.

I am a jewel.

And a jewel rarely comes out of the earth.

The wooden box was like a bed which swayed with the song, or a boat on a sea of bodies. They were human bodies, sons of Adam and daughters of Eve. They advanced line after line, and column after column. The men's heads were not shaven. Their hair was thick and dark, covering the backs of their necks. The women had long, black, flowing hair, and their eyes were big and looked upwards to the sky. Their feet trod on the ground with a single step, and their breathing mingled together in one breath, like the whisper of the wind, like her mother's voice singing to her in the cradle.

– Hou, hou, sleep my sweet, sleep.

The trees rose to the sky, and their branches swayed to the same rhythm. The children on the bank of the river waved the flies away from their faces, lifted their eyes up, turned round and took hold of the bottoms of each other's *gallabeyas*. Then they circled behind one another, singing.

– Hou, hou, sleep sweet child, sleep.

The cow stopped turning the water-wheel, stretched its neck upwards and lowed in rhyme with the song. The goat and the donkey, the little puppy lifting its head from the dustbin, the child sucking at its mother's breast on the pavement, the cats, the stray dogs, the tufts of dry yellow grass over the bare ground all sang her mother's song.

– Hou, hou, sleep sweet child, sleep.

She opened her eyes in the wooden box and saw the face of her mother shining in the dark. Her eyes were covered with a film of moisture like tears which neither dried nor dropped out. They shone from a distance in the dark sky like the morning star. Millions of voices sang a lullaby, millions of voices as soft as the rustle of the wind in the leaves of the trees.

13 *The Innocence of the Devil*

The big gate closed after Ganat was carried out. Its hinges creaked like an ancient water-wheel, and the black iron posts trembled. The walls of the palace also trembled, the earth beneath, the tops of the trees, the wires stretched out above the fence. Birds flew off in all directions.

He was standing near the trunk of a tree, wrapped in his long white robe. His hair was thick and black, his eyes big and steady, filled with an imprisoned tear, like a fine mist which seemed to shiver when the gate closed. Under the mist his eye remained steadfast, flaming with a dark light. The links of the iron chain clicked against one another, and the huge lock swayed from side to side, gave a final jump like a last surge of life, and then came to a standstill as though dead.

A faint light fell on his face. His nose from the side was straight, not like his father's nose. His lips were slightly parted, and his breath smelt like that of children.

On his upper lip grew soft hairs. His robe was open at the neck, torn at the back, showing an old deep wound under the shoulder blade.

The sky was black without moon or stars. The air was heavy, loaded with smoke and the feeling of defeat, the smell of gunpowder and burning oil. The tops of the trees were immobile like dead phantoms.

His eyes moved over, to and fro, searching for something, for a drop of light in the ocean of black. The black clouds were a thick cloak carrying dust and sand. His wide-open eyes wandered through the universe with a deep yearning. He stood upright on his legs, sleeping, whenever he needed to sleep, in a standing position.

Suddenly he saw her cutting through the clouds. The first thing he saw was her eyes shining from afar. The more he looked into them the more they seemed to shine. They looked at him from above the horizon the way his mother's eyes looked at him when he walked along the road. She would be standing there to take a last glance at him before he disappeared. Her voice would follow him from afar as she read to him a poem she had written for him the night before.

   – I love you
     Because you are the only one amongst the slaves
     Who refused to kneel
     Who said no
     I saw you walk

With your head upright and your hair so dense,
so black.
Covering distances in the dark
Amidst the desert storm
And smiling
No one can take your smile away from you
Nor take away your slim outline
Your body never bends
Your head never bends down, too.

When Ganat walked by his side he listened to her voice. It was like listening to an ancient melody. Hand in hand they ran to school. The bell rang and the boys shouted. The trees shook to the rhythm of their voices, and the sun's rays danced between their high branches.

He saw her jumping, touching the branches with her fingertips, touching the rays of the sun as they dropped. Then her body would fall back to earth. She landed flat on her face, her nose and mouth choked with dust. She stood up, dusted her clothes and threw back her head, and laughed. Her laugh floated around her head like circles of light.

She started to jump again. He jumped with her. He touched the high branches and the rays of sun with his fingertips just as she did, then fell back into the depths of the sea, and they swam, she like a silver fish and he by her side just as quick. They raced one another under the water, dived deep down to the depths. Their fingertips touched pearls and coral reefs, red, and green, and blue, and yellow plants, all the colours of the rainbow. They laughed with voices that danced like the waves, that rose up and up to reach the moon and kiss its face.

He reached out and took her hand. She whispered in his ear:

– Eblis?

He whispered in her ear under the water:

– I am not a devil, Ganat.

I am not Satan

And I'm not an angel.

My mother is sad. And my sister is Nefissa.[1]

I am human

Just like you

And my heart is open.

His voice flowed into his ears as he walked along. I am human and my heart is open. His eyes filled with tears. His feet were naked, and the tips of his toes pressed down on the earth. He was afraid to tread on the leaves, to tread with his shoes on his land. She took off her shoes and held them in her hand. She threw them into the river and clapped with glee. The soles of her feet felt the soil. She loved the feel of the earth on the soles of her feet. She laughed and ran across the water. Her dress was white, made of silk. On the sleeves were flowers made of lace that flew

[1] Here the word means precious.

around her like wings. She fluttered her wings and
rose in the air like a white butterfly. She flew over the
wires on the fence and hovered beneath the clouds.
He saw her in the distance like a white arrow, cutting
into the clouds and disappearing, then reappearing in
the distance, like the morning star.

He was standing near the fence, his eyes fixed on
her, his arms raised up in the air. The tips of his fingers
could almost touch her. He rose on his toes as high as
he could, climbed up the fence like a child climbing
up to his mother's breast. Her voice came to him from
nowhere.

– Where is my son, o Zahra, mother of justice and
mercy?

Her arms reached out to him as he climbed up over
the fence, lifting his body up and leaping in the air.
But the earth kept pulling him back again. He fell
back with his eyes on her. Dust filled his nose and his
mouth.

He stood up again, dusted off his robe. He jumped
again, one jump after another. He kept jumping and
falling back, jumping and falling back, but he never
gave up.

The fence was very high and the wires made it even
higher. There were splinters of glass on it with sharp
edges like nails. The edges between the stone were
sharp and stuck out. His hands were grazed, and the
skin was being pulled off them. Thin threads of blood

coursed their way over the skin like fine arteries. His white robe soaked up the blood. It caught on a sharp edge and was torn. It fell from his body and curled up on the ground near the fence, like a blood-covered embryo dropping out of its mother.

He stood there, his body naked except for his underpants. His face was bathed in moonlight. He stared at the red-spotted robe as though it were a dead child lying there. Perhaps he had died as he stood there, or was living the last moments before death.

In the very last leap before the soul leaves the body he suddenly felt very light. His body tried to catch hold of his soul before it escaped, as it floated some distance away from him. He stretched out his hands and took hold of it. His hands were covered in blood, and most of the skin had come off them. His face was white as a sheet, drained of blood. His eyes were large and full of light.

And in this last moment before death his body rose up and touched his soul. He held on to it with his fingers and his toes. He kept holding on with all his strength and his soul flew up with him high over the fence. His arms and his legs fluttered like wings. The bones of his back stood out like a skeleton without flesh. Below his shoulder-blade was a deep wound.

He flew higher and higher up into the sky. His body gleamed in the light like an arrow. His black head plunged deep into the clouds and disappeared in the dark spaces, only to reappear somewhere else like a distant star, looking down on the city with the morning star by its side.

The eyes gazed up at them from behind the iron bars, half-closed in a kind of sleep. They were the eyes of human beings, sons of Adam and daughters of Eve. Their pupils looked through a transparent layer of water like glass. Their robes were white and wide, a sign of madness, and around each waist was a narrow belt. It was enough for their eyes to meet for the contagion to be transferred from one to the other.

The men had their heads closely shaven in conformity with the instructions of the Director. Their faces were covered in lank, lifeless hair which hung down over their chests, and their heads were swathed in veils. They kept their arms crossed over their breasts, and their hands under their cheeks. Their lips were always closed, and not a sound emerged from them. They looked at the sky in silence, without hope, without despair, nothing. All there was to see was the white light which covered the face of the moon like snow. A sad, silent light which seemed to hang in space and express nothing, not disillusion, or expectation, or a silent prayer, nothing at all.

He was standing at the window of the male ward. His ears were strained to catch any sound, hoping to hear something, to hear someone call out to him. Even the wind had ceased its whispering. There was no movement, not the slightest sound.

His eyes opened wider and his black pupils circled in the dark. He was standing clothed in his wide *gallabeya*, tall and broad-shouldered. His head was wrapped in seven layers of a gauze-like material, one layer over the other. At the top protruded the black feather like a cockscomb. His long, white beard hung down over his chest. His face was white and square indicating his noble ancestry which was related, far back, to that of the King. His nose was a big cart-ilaginous hook which proved that he was his father's son and no one else's. His heart was heavy and the air around him was suffocating. His chest rose and fell, and his breath came in gasps. His eyes were round and the pupils kept going round like black beads.

He lifted his nose up in the air and walked down between the beds as he used to do between lines of soldiers standing row upon row. Thousands of rows and thousands of faces indistinguishable from one another. Amongst all these faces all he could see was one face, his face reflected in their eyes, on a surface that was like still, stagnant water. Above his head rose the feather like a needle, and in his hand he held the sword he had inherited from his father. His voice resounded in his ears like that of his grandfather.

– Obedience, you slaves.

Here I am the one who gives orders.

Whoever disobeys

Will have his head cut off.

The soldiers lifted their guns and shouted in unison:

– Long live! Long live! Forever.

The word *forever* echoed in his ears. His body shivered with ecstasy. He nodded his head in satisfaction. Since he was a child he had longed, deep down, to be eternal. He looked up at the Pyramid of Khoufou, and saw himself sitting at its apex. Around him were the planets and the stars and he shone brightly amidst them. On his breast were rows of medals, and over his head was a crown, with two long horns curling forwards. Over the horns he carried the disc of the sun. He climbed on the shoulders of the boys at school and shouted out:

– I! I am the greatest! The greatest! -test! -test!

He was crowing like a cock and the soldiers roared back:

– Long live! Long live!

Bullets dropped from the sky like rain, and bombs fell from the bellies of black eagles. The Khamaseen winds blew loaded with dust, and particles of sand, with a smell of gunpowder and burning oil. Smoke filled up the world.

Bodies flew through the air and burst into fragments of flesh. They were the bodies of human beings, of the sons of Adam and the daughters of Eve. Men were recognised by their fingers, by the index finger and the thumb. Women by their breasts.

He looked at her out of the corner of his eye as he walked down between the lines. His chest rose and fell under the armoured plate. The two breasts shivered and shook under the dancer's dress. He winked at her, as though he had moved with the times. None of the soldiers saw him do it and none of the bullets ever hit his chest. He always returned home safely. At night he would wake up, creep out of bed and put on his mask. His wife would open one eye and close the other.

In the morning he would discover his underpants burnt to ashes in the basin, and in his chest he would find the wound under the armoured plate, piercing from the front of his chest to the back, yet without a single drop of blood. The bed-sheet would be clean and white, as white as the colour of death.

He put on the armour, hid the opening in his flesh under a layer of steel. His shoes had a high neck made of tiger-skin and a thick square heel under which was nailed an iron horseshoe. He stamped with his shoes on the tarmac road, stamped on his land when he walked, crushed leaves under his iron heels, knocked the right one against the left in a salute, lifted his leg high in the air like a wooden stick. His voice echoed in his ears like the whistle of the wind.

– I! I! I am the one who gives orders. Forever!
Forever!

There was a deep silence. It was a prolonged,
strange, heavy silence. The soldiers were standing upright in rows. No one shouted out. No voice said: Long
Live! They stood row upon row, line after line. They
had their backs to him and their faces to the wall. No
one turned round to look at him.

His eyes opened wide, his pupils bulged. He looked
round to the left and to the right. People walked with
half-closed eyes. Their faces were long and white and
their breath came in gasps. No one recognised his face,
no one paid any attention to him. The waters of the
Nile flowed on oblivious. Black bodies floated on the
river without looking at him. Their eyes gazed into
space, filled with emptiness.

He crossed the street with a heavy step. A car almost
ran over him. His body shook, and the turban with
the feather fell off. His shaven head shone in the light.
The driver braked suddenly, and the car came to a
stop with a jerk. A head looked out of the window and
shouted out:

– Can't you see, you ass?

– Don't you know who I am, ass yourself?

– Who could you be? God?

– Yes, exactly. I'm God but I'm not wearing my
official uniform.

He felt his uncovered head, then noticed the feather

being carried in the wind along the shore. He ran after it, trying to catch it before it fell in the river. He put the turban back on his head, with the feather at the top.

He found her on the pavement, curled up on herself like an embryo. A child was sucking at one breast, and a kitten at the other. She looked into his face for a long moment. Her eyes were big and black with a film of moisture over their surface. She noticed his old *gallabeya* and the plastic slippers on his feet. She pushed her hand into the pocket of her robe and gave him a *piastre*.

– Don't you know who I am?

I! I! Everyone used to give me a royal salute. I am high up, above everyone else.

He walked along the street stopping everyone who passed by and saying:

– Do you know who I am? I . . . I . . . am above everyone. Everybody gives me a royal salute . . . royal . . . everyone . . . kneels down.

His eyes kept looking around him as he walked in the dark. His voice rang in his ears as he repeated *everybody kneels*. The heads of the trees bowed down under the wind as though bowing to him. Long lines of soldiers kneeled on the ground in prayer. He nodded his head with satisfaction, walked with a slow step, his nose held high up in the air. He climbed up the steps to the male ward, and walked between the rows of beds. They were all asleep, their eyes closed, their bodies stretched out on their beds without movement. He nodded his head and smiled. Order reigned in the world, and everyone lay prostrate before him.

Suddenly his eyes lit upon the empty bed. The smile on his face froze at once. His eyes opened wide and the pupils bulged. He shook his head in disbelief. He bent down and looked under the bed.

– Where's Eblis?

The light of the moon fell on the sheet which was stretched taut over the bed like death. The pillow was empty, and the empty pillowcase shone white as snow. His body shivered as though with cold. An icy wind blew in from the window. A black hair on the empty pillowcase shone in the moonlight. It writhed with a visible movement as though a spirit were alive in it, then flew away carried by a draught. He caught it between his thumb and index finger, and brought it close up to his eyes. He shook his head several times and said:

– Impossible.

He lifted up his face and the light fell on his eyes. The whites of his eyes appeared large, and over them lay a transparent mist like water. The small pupils vibrated, turning on themselves and shaking with every movement of his head.

– Impossible.

– Eblis can never die.

His voice echoed as he repeated: Never die! His body shivered, and his voice changed, became the voice of another man, with a hoarse croak like that of his grandfather before he died. His feet were heavy as he walked in the darkness. The shadows of the trees moved like phantoms. He crushed the leaves under his feet as he walked. He could hear them moan like the faint moaning of a dying cat. He stopped for a moment, and strained his ears. He could hear footsteps. He turned round cautiously and whispered:

– Eblis?!

He could see him tall and dark, standing upright behind him. Only one or two feet separated them. His lips parted to let out a deep breath. His arms reached towards him, but they closed on empty air, just as though he touched a shadow lying on the ground. Every time he moved towards it, it moved away.

– Eblis! Come here! Answer me, boy!

Silence enveloped the world except for the faint whistling of something like the wind, coming from afar. The leaves on the trees shivered with a slow movement. A leaf could be heard as it landed on the ground. He watched it float down gradually, reach the ground, turn over several times before it came to rest as though lifeless.

He bent his head. His nose hung down over his

beard. In his ears echoed the long whistle which extended through the night, the million voices which made up the silence of the night. The silence resounded in his ears like the roar of the waterfall and the roar melted into a single word which sounded like the whistling of the wind.

– Eblis?!

He held his head between his hands. He could see the phantom by his side holding its head between its hands. He whispered as though any sound could make it disappear.

– Come! Do not go away!

The echo of his voice came back to him with the movement of the air. His eyes opened wide under the light and filled up with tears.

– How can you leave me alone like this?

O my son!

The word *son* echoed in his father's voice as it did when he called out in the night as he lay dying. He leaned his back against a tree. His chest rose and fell. He clasped his arms around it, squatted on the ground and curled up around himself.

He glimpsed a dark phantom by his side curled around itself with its back to a tree. He moved his head closer to it and whispered:

– You made the world so rich for me, Eblis.

He lifted his eyes and looked through his tears at the wide-open spaces. A tear rolled down from the corner of his eyes. He let it fall, did not wipe it with his sleeve.

— Forgive me, my son. I know I used to wake you up so often from your sleep, and tell you to get up immediately, to go round whispering in people's ears. I wrote three books against you, and denied you the right to answer them.

He wiped his eyes with his sleeve and bent his head to his knees.

— I am responsible for our defeat, my son!

He who has authority is responsible.

But the world was upside down.

He who is responsible for what happens is made out to be innocent.

And the people who are under our rule are put on trial.

The generals get medals.

The soldiers die.

He lifted his head and gazed at the sky. There was not a drop of light. No moon, no stars. The heads of the trees were motionless, and the wind was silent. The light in the Head Nurse's room was extinguished, and her window was shut. The palace was plunged in darkness. His eyes stared into nothing.

— In the court they declared me innocent and made you the scapegoat.

The word *scapegoat* rang out loudly, in the night, like a piece of stone thrown into a dark cesspit. The darkness moved in circles, in big circles surrounding smaller circles with a black hole in the middle, like the mouth of a pit.

– Forgive me, my son.

You are innocent.

He stood up suddenly as he pronounced the word *innocent*. The dark waters ceased their movement, and the world turned into one solid, black, marble slab. The word *innocent* dropped on to the marble slab shining like a white *piastre*, and ringing loudly in the silence with a sound like silver.

– Innocent!

The ringing in his ears went higher and higher, as he walked along inside the fence. The fence was high with wire along the top. The clouds were black. They split open to let through a disc that shone in the dark with a white light.

He glimpsed him under the light curled up like an embryo in its mother's womb. His body was white, as white as cotton, torn over his chest, and under the shoulder-blade, and covered with red spots like blood.

He buried his head in the cotton robe trying to smell it, like a father smelling the odour of his dead son. His voice sobbed every now and then repeating:

– Innocent! Innocent!

The echo of his voice made the fence and the wire tremble. The birds woke up and flew into the air. The iron gate shook and with it the iron chain and the black lock. The shaking spread to the grounds and the walls of the palace. The echo went on like the sound of wind shaking the doors and the windows. The heads of the trees, the tall buildings, the wire on the top of walls, the towers, the five-star hotels, the forts, the palaces, the prisons, the domes of churches, the minarets of mosques, the telegraph poles, all shook.

– Innocent! Innocent!

Whistles sounded everywhere and bells rang. The Director appeared wearing his nightgown with a whistle in his mouth. Behind him came the male nurses in their white aprons, carrying ropes in their hands. Following them were policemen wearing brass helmets and holding torches. Stray dogs, cats, beggars and newspaper vendors. Tanks rolled out with guns showing from their turrets. The bells of the churches rang and the bells of schools. Microphones on the tops of minarets cried out. The women *you you'ed* or shrieked at the tops of their voices, and the *you yous* themselves became like shrieks. The Khamaseen winds filled the world with dust and sand. Soldiers marched in endless rows and columns. At the front was the General and at his side was his Majesty the King and the rulers, and those who decided what should be done and what should not. Their faces were all white and washed of all their sins. They smiled like innocent children, and around their necks were flowers. The flowers were dead, hanging from iron spits curled into hoops around the neck.

They found him lying on his back close to the fence, wearing his white robe. His head was closely shaven in accordance with the orders given by the Director. His eyes were open, gazing at the sky. The pupils were black and fixed, staring into space. His lips were slightly parted as though in a smile, with a slight twist of the mouth to one side. His face was square and white, bathed in light. The black feather kept shifting over the ground as though there were still some life in it.